MICHAEL MERRIAM

TERROR AT TIERRA DE COBRE

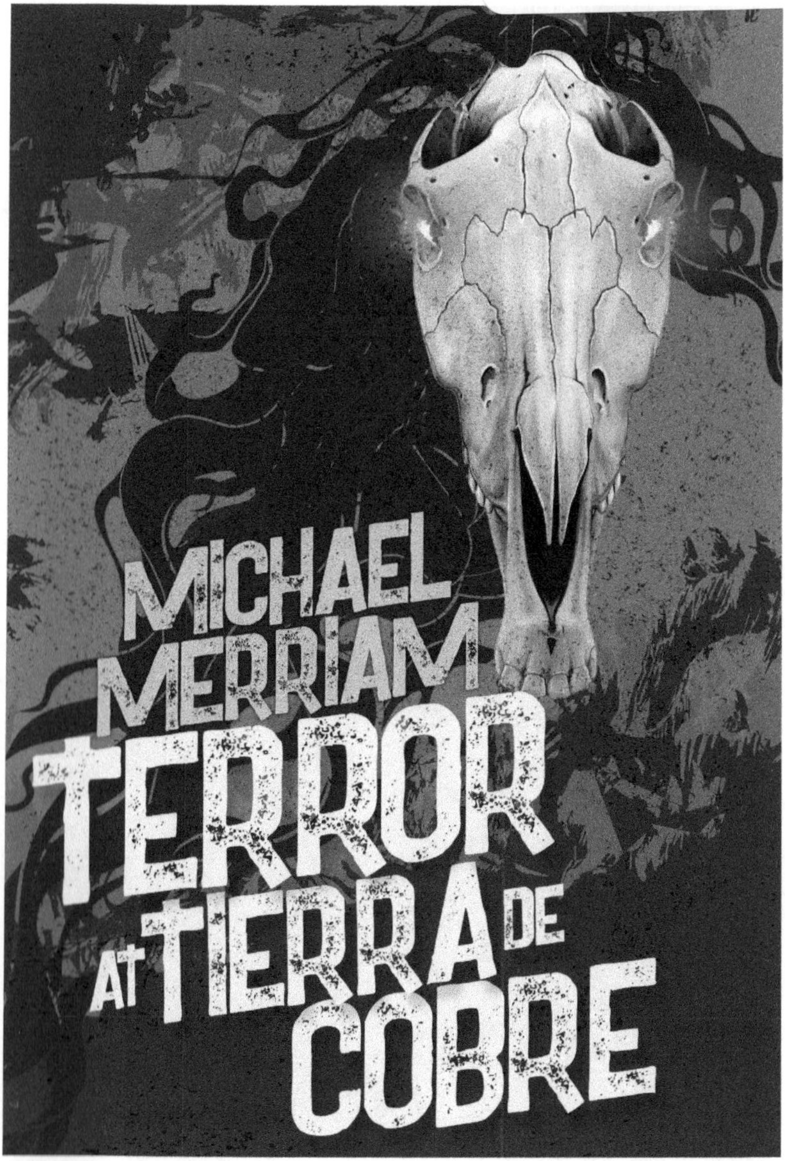

ALSO BY MICHAEL MERRIAM

Six Guns & Sorcery Series:

Charming Mayhem: A Six Guns & Sorcery Omnibus by Michael Merriam with Sherry Merriam

Queen of Swords Press Titles by Michael Merriam:

Last Car to Annwn Station

TERROR AT TIERRA DE COBRE

MICHAEL MERRIAM

INTRODUCTION

Our careers are never what we think they are going to be.

If you had told me as a new author I would be writing a series of books set in an alternative American West - an American West that never was but could have been - I would have shaken my head, mumbled something about swords and sorcery, and ambled back to my laptop.

The thing is, I am firmly grounded in the stories (one could even say, the myth) of the American West, be it books, the big screen, or the small screen. I grew up in Oklahoma and knew direct descendants of men and women who lived in those times. My grandfather lied to a recruiting sergeant, joined the army at sixteen, and rode in the mounted cavalry. *The Wild Wild West* television show and comic books like *Weird Western Tales* taught me that those stories could be fantastical or supernatural.

One day, a publisher offered me *money* to write a supernatural western novella. I wrote it. And I found I wanted to tell more tales about those characters and the world they existed in. I loved crafting stories in the setting while examining all the myths and folklore pulp stories and the big screen taught us. The truth about the West is better and deeper. Weirder.

Now, here we are, the fifth novella of the series (and the first published by the excellent Queen of Swords Press) set in an American West filled with magic, monsters, and steampunk gadgets. Each book is a standalone, so do not fear diving in. These are all new characters to the setting in a new story.

Welcome to the world of Six Guns & Sorcery. Saddle up, reader, and ride with us.

CHAPTER
ONE

The women of Tierra de Cobre stood in the town square watching as a dozen men, all mercenaries, rode out, heading for the pond a handful of miles from the town, near the spring that fed the creek and brought water to their homes. Most of the women, tired and bedraggled, turned back toward their homes.

"Do you think they will…" Maria Garcia could not bring herself to finish the statement. She clutched her rosary with one hand. The other touched the butt of the Colt Navy she wore. Her husband's spare revolver. She feared that he didn't need it anymore. This group of bravos would vanish the same as her Esteban.

"Die?"

Maria turned to glance at the speaker. Charlotte Klaski taught the village school children. Her husband Richard ran the local newspaper and was one of the first to go looking for the missing men of Tierra de Cobre. First, the miners never returned home, then the town marshal and his deputy vanished searching for them. After that, there were others, more townsfolk and now hired mercenaries.

Charlotte shrugged and pulled her red hair back, bound it up with a bit of ribbon. "Probably."

"Best pray they don't," Anna-Beth Carson answered. She idly brushed a strand of her limp brown hair away from her thin pale face. Anna-Beth had stepped into the role vacated by her missing husband. The Mayor of Tierra de Cobre had led the doomed search party with Richard Klaski and Maria's husband Esteban, proprietor of the town's little stable. "I'd guess the word will be getting out. I doubt we'd be able to hire another group."

"Well, we'd best pray extra hard, ladies." Temperance was the oldest woman in town at somewhere on the other side of seventy. A sturdy dark-skinned woman wearing a faded blue blouse and white skirt with a cook's apron, Maria knew that, despite Anne-Beth being the mayor's wife, Temperance was the town's real leader. "Best pray extra hard, indeed."

Charlotte snorted. "I'm done praying. Praying didn't do Preacher Wilkes nor any of our menfolk any good. Didn't save the Padre and his blue robe guide either. God don't hear our prayers anymore."

"Charlotte! How could you say such a thing?" Maria gripped her rosary tighter. In her mind, she asked Mary to intercede on their behalf.

Charlotte nodded toward the fading sounds of horse hooves on hard dirt. "You know those men aren't coming back, just like the last group. Just like our men never came back."

Maria peered into the dust cloud the mercenaries' horses raised. "We should go to the pond ourselves."

"You ready to fight whatever's there?" Temperance asked.

"I'd rather not even think about it," Anna-Beth said.

"Well, all of us might vanish into nothing soon

enough." Charlotte sighed and wiped her hands on her sides. "I need a bath and my bed. We should all get some rest while we await the fate of our brave would-be heroes ."

Anna-Beth sighed. "Amen to that."

Charlotte and Anna-Beth slowly turned and walked away, leaving Maria alone with Temperance. The words tumbled out of Maria's mouth, "Do you think they're right? Are we abandoned by God?"

"Well, I guess we'll find out soon." Temperance gave Maria's shoulder a little pat before walking away. In the distance, the sound of gunfire filled the air; intense at first, it became a sporadic trickle and then, finally, nothing.

Maria clutched her rosary in her left hand. *"En el nombre del Padre, y del Hijo..."*

∼

MARIA GLANCED at the group of women gathered in the darkness. A few held torches, looking down the main street. Temperance, a shotgun cradled in her arms, stood next to Maria.

Anna-Beth's niece Daisy, acting as lookout, climbed into the belfry of the Catholic mission as she had every night since the last men of Tierra de Cobre went searching for their brothers and friends, never to return. The teenager had raised the alarm, summoning the women into the night.

A lone horse trotted up the dirt road, its rider slumped over the saddle. The horse walked into town on wobbly legs, and its nostrils flared, eyes rolling in fear. The rider fell from the saddle to the dusty street with a wet thump. A smear of blood gleamed on the saddle, evidence of his gruesome injuries. Anna-Beth captured the animal's reins and managed to calm it.

Charlotte stepped up and poked the body with her rifle. It stayed limp on the ground. "Well, I suppose that's the answer to our prayers."

Several of the women began to wail and cry out. Temperance turned to the gathered group. "Hush! Hush, the lot of you! This is no time for this caterwauling and carrying on."

Rachel Owens stepped forward. Maria narrowed her eyes at the sturdy brunette. Maria considered her neighbor level-headed and fearless, but lately Rachel proved the most vocal in favor of quitting their claims to the copper mine.

"We should leave," Rachel said. "We should abandon this godforsaken town. Whatever's out there, we can't stop it. If it comes for us, it will slaughter us all."

The dead body of the rider rose to his feet, swaying. Charlotte scampered back with a shriek. The bloody corpse turned its pale, lifeless eyes on the women and its mouth opened. "Give them to us," it said in a raspy voice. "Give the rest to us, or we shall take them. Give them over and join us, sisters. Join—"

Temperance fired her shotgun into the middle of the dead man's chest. The animated corpse fell to the dusty street. "Quiet down!" Temperance tried to regain control of the panicked women. They shuffled nervously, ready to bolt at the next sign of trouble, but gave the old woman their attention. "If some of y'all want to run, I would not blame you, but I'm too damned old to be running, and I'm not giving up my claim."

Charlotte sighed. "Temperance, I know, but that thing, it's taken or killed everyone we've sent."

Something clicked in Maria's mind, a crazy idea.

"Every man we've sent," Maria said. She kept her eyes on the corpse. Dead things should stay dead, but she worried this one might rise again. It lay still, so she hoped whatever kept it moving must be over and done. With a sigh, she looked away. The other women stared at her in confusion before realization dawned on them. "Every man we've sent," she repeated. "So we stop sending men."

Anna-Beth shook her head. "Are you daft, girl? Do you think you'll find, I don't know, mercenary women? Women soldiers?"

"I don't know." Maria shrugged her shoulders. "I don't know, but I'm willing to try."

"There's a few out there," Temperance said.

"Women of ill repute," Charlotte chuckled.

Rachel Owens frowned. "We've got our own of that ilk."

Maria shook her head. "No, not prostitutes. I mean adventuresses."

"I don't care what you call them," Anna-Beth replied. "Can we find them, and will they help?"

A scream arose from the crowd of women as they scattered like startled sparrows seeking sanctuary. Maria half turned. The corpse climbed to its feet as if pulled by strings. It lurched toward her. She took a step backward and drew her pistol. Lining up her shot, she put the lead bullet through the shambling corpse's head. It fell back and withered into dust.

Maria turned to Temperance. "I'll ride to Magdalena." She looked around at the remaining women. "I hope at least one or two of you will ride with me."

"You've no business in that place alone," Charlotte said.

"You'll come with me then?" Maria wanted others to ride with her and wanted company on the trip badly, but she was just beginning to trust Charlotte, Anne-Beth, and the other white women. They had always been pleasant to her because her husband owned a business, but this almost friendship was new. Maria was unsure of them.

"Of course. Honestly, I'm more likely to get them to help anyway." Charlotte gave Maria a sympathetic smile. "I'm sorry Maria, but you know it's true."

"I'll come." Anna-Beth's voice trembled. "My cousin Florence lives in Magdalena. I can ask her for a place to stay."

Temperance gave them an approving look. "Then it's settled. We'll get you three on the road at dawn."

CHAPTER
TWO

The young Apache woman knelt in the rough red dirt of the high mesa and studied the three riders below. She had traveled to their little village, drawn by the call of the curse, needing to bring the monster to an end. Or at least to trap it again, even if it meant she would become the keeper of the curse, like her grandmother before her.

Shifting the battered Springfield rifle in her arms, she watched the women. Her initial impression was that they looked like soft village women who had never lived alone on the edges of everything. She snorted and laughed at herself. They were strong in their way, or else the land would have long since taken them. This land held no mercy for the weak and foolish: they became nothing but bones and dust quick enough.

Do not underestimate them, she thought. *And do not overestimate yourself. Again.* Overestimating herself ended with her trapped in the brothels of El Paso. She frowned at the memory of her violent, bloody escape.

She sat back on her heels, the wind blowing the too-big

blouse and faded skirt she wore. The three women carried only their weapons and what they needed to make camp, so they were not fleeing the dark one. She would follow them. Follow to divine their business, to study and see if they remained free-willed or part of the darkness slowly spreading from the mining town of Tierra de Cobre. If free women, she would quietly protect them as they crossed the badlands. But she would deal with them swiftly if she determined they were dark daughters carrying the curse into the world.

Given the previous night's events, she suspected they were free of the beast's power. Kira had watched from afar as the group of armed men rode to their doom. The beast and its forces cut some down. They were the lucky ones. The others were now the walking dead thralls of the thing dwelling at the pond.

She waited until the women rounded a bend on the wagon trail they followed before rising and moving. The track would take them to Magdalena, the largest town for miles. She would pass them to the south and take a position near the clearwater spring nearly midway to Magdalena. They would likely camp there for the night, allowing her to observe them more closely.

She touched the copper knife, hidden by her too-large skirts, reassuring herself it still rested in its leather sheath. She'd visited her *shiwóyé's* isolated camp just long enough for her grandmother to entrust the weapon into her keeping. Her grandmother had told her that she would soon be gone, that the knife and the battle against the rising darkness would become Kira's burden.

She snorted softly to herself. Her grandmother couldn't even tell her how to use the knife when the dark one rose to spread its control across the world, only that it was the key to ending the monster. Grandmother told her the *Hactcin,* the creators of her people, crafted the weapon to counter the beast and promised they would guide her hand when the time came.

She had little use for spirits from old stories, but the blade was all she carried to turn back the dark. As with everything else in her life, she'd need to figure it out while trying to survive.

❦

MAGDALENA, Maria thought, *is what Tierra de Cobre could be if it had a railroad stop. And more of everything.* It was at least four times larger than Tierra de Cobre.

The three women rode their tired horses down the dusty main street, with the pack mule trailing behind on his lead rope. Four saloons, a hotel, a dry goods store, a bank, and other businesses lined the main street. The town marshal's office sat centrally in the street, with a low adobe jail next to it. A creaky windmill filled a water trough at the end of the street near the small stockyards and livery stable.

Maria studied the townspeople going about their business. Most of them cast the three women hostile glances. She could feel the anger coming from multiple corners. She should have expected this. The first group to try and help Tierra de Cobre came from Magdalena. Those men vanished too, disappearing into whatever hell haunted her home.

"We should split up," Anna-Beth said. "I'll go talk to Florence about staying with her."

"I'll take the animals and see to their care." Maria swung down from her saddle.

Charlotte frowned. "I'll talk to my friends at the newspaper and then check in with the marshal. "

"Do we think anyone will help us again?" Anna-Beth asked.

"If the looks we're getting mean anything, no," Maria said. "But we didn't come for the help of the folks of Magdalena."

"Agreed," Anna-Beth replied. "Let's be about this."

Maria took the lead for the mule from Anna-Beth and the reins for the other horses. Anna-Beth walked toward the interior of the town, homes lining dirt streets. Charlotte strolled toward the newspaper office.

Maria walked the horses and mule toward the water trough under the windmill. She kept her head up and eyes moving while watering the animals. She noted the dark-skinned woman standing in the wide-open double doors of the livery stable. The woman wore weathered men's trail garb: a wide-brimmed hat, a duster over her shirt and trousers. Her boots were worn. She carried a double barrel shotgun strapped across her back and a revolver cross-draw. She leaned against the building, regarding Maria with curious eyes, as if taking her measure. She looked exactly like the type of tough fighting woman Maria wanted to hire. Maria was thinking about how to approach her when an angry voice made her turn around.

"You have some nerve coming back here." Maria recognized the man as a local preacher, one who rained fire and brimstone from the pulpit. She couldn't remember his name.

"I don't see how it's any of your business," she replied.

The preacher walked briskly toward her, his face clouded with anger. "You've brought down whatever curse Tierra de Cobre suffers on the good folks here in Magdalena. We'll send no more men into your devil's den."

Maria blinked at him. "Devil's den?"

"Gather up your friends and leave before nightfall or

face the wrath of the Lord, you little witch!" The man's eyes bugged out and she thought he might spit on her in his frenzy.

Maria tightened her grip on the reins of the animals and took a half-step backward. "What is wrong with you?"

"You've been warned. Leave Magdalena and never return."

The preacher turned on his heel and strode away without another word, back toward the center of town. Various bystanders who'd stopped to watch the confrontation returned to their business. The town marshal, an older man, stood in front of his office. He peered past the retreating preacher toward Maria. She wondered if he would come to harass her next. She returned to watering her animals when he didn't move toward her. "What the hell?" she muttered.

"They're scared."

Maria looked up, startled. The woman who stood in the livery stable's open doors just moments before now stood beside her. For someone carrying so many weapons, the woman moved quiet as a cat. She stammered a little as she responded, "I'm sorry. I don't understand."

"Town's seen some trouble recently. Which is why I strolled over to chat with you."

Maria extended her hand. "Maria. Maria Garcia."

The woman took her hand in a cool, firm grip. Maria noted the rough calluses, a sign of someone who worked with their hands daily. "Ophelia Virginia Barnett. Tell me, Maria Garcia, do you and your friends need a place to stay?"

"We might be staying with my friend's cousin," Maria said. "Otherwise, I don't know. I suppose the hotel if they'll take us." Maria nodded toward the street as the townsfolk watched her. "I feel we might not be welcome."

"I reckon you might not be," Ophelia agreed. "But the preacher-man is right about one thing. You'd best be gone from town or under cover before the sun goes down. If this friend's cousin doesn't work out, come back here. I can make it right for you and yours to sleep at the stables tonight."

"Like we're hiding? Hiding from what?" Something in Ophelia's tone suggested it wasn't just angry townsfolk that she was referring to.

Ophelia gave her a little humorless smile. "Well, now, Maria Garcia, I don't know what trouble you're facing back home, but just take my word, this is not something you want to meet, no indeed."

Maria followed Ophelia's gaze up the street to a lone woman standing before the marshal's office. She wore a long black dress with a high collar. A black veil covered her face, and Maria thought she might be holding a rosary, though it was hard to tell from this distance.

Ophelia tipped her hat to Maria. "Now, if you will excuse me, Maria Garcia, I've business to attend. Remember what I said. Find yourself a place to hole up by sundown."

Maria watched as Ophelia approached the other woman. They talked briefly before turning toward a side street leading to the local homes. Maria bit her bottom lip. She needed to speak with Anna-Beth and Charlotte about these women.

"I--I'm sorry, Maria. Florence was fine with you staying, but Chet...well, he's...um..." Anna-Beth stared down at the ground, twisting the fabric of her dress in her hands.

Maria, Anna-Beth, and Charlotte stood before Anna-

Beth's cousin's home. They'd unloaded Anna-Beth and Charlotte's bags and packs from the horses and mule.

"He's a pig-headed piece of shit," Charlotte snarled.

Anna-Beth gasped. "Charlotte! He's just—he has strong feelings about Mexicans."

Maria frowned at Anna-Beth's words. "It's fine," Maria finally said, willing to suffer even this indignity if it helped their cause in the end. "I'll stay in the stables or set up a camp outside of town."

Charlotte turned to her. "It's not fine! If his feelings about Mexicans are so strong, he should reconsider living some place called 'The New Mexico Territory.'"

"Charlotte!" Anna-Beth glanced over her shoulder at her cousin's home.

"Let's try the hotel," Charlotte said.

Maria shook her head. "We need to save our money for the hired guns. Anyway, given the feelings of folks around here, I'm not sure they'd rent us a room."

Charlotte grimaced. "Nobody would even look at me in the newspaper office. I was told me no one would hire with us."

Maria frowned at Anna-Beth. "I met a woman today. She was armed to the teeth. Shotgun, revolver, knives. She told me we need to be off the street by sundown."

"Trouble?" Anna-Beth glanced up at the sun.

"I'm sure," Maria said. "But I'm more interested in this woman. She struck me as the type of woman we're looking for, a woman used to trouble. There was another woman with her."

"Another walking arsenal?" Charlotte asked.

"No. I think she might be a nun."

"A nun?" The disbelief came through clearly in Charlotte's voice.

"Maria shrugged. "She dressed like one and carried

what looked like a rosary, though not of an order I recognized." Maria turned to Anne-Beth. "We don't need trouble right here. Give me the animals. I'll see to them. You two stay here, and tomorrow, we'll start searching for help."

Anna-Beth reached out to Maria as Charlotte started lifting their bags. "I'm so sorry, Maria."

Maria squeezed Anna-Beth's offered hand before leading all the animals back toward the livery stable. "Guess I'm staying with you tonight," she muttered at them.

CHAPTER

THREE

Maria rolled over again, trying to find a comfortable spot. After spending the last two nights sleeping rough in a bedroll on the trail between Tierra de Cobre and Magdalena, she thought settling into a nest of saddle blankets on the dry hay would be a luxury, but the smell of horses and mules, sweat and shit kept her restless. And the buzzing flies. So many buzzing flies. She'd also been looking forward to sleeping in something other than her trail clothes.

The livery stable owner shrugged and spat on the dirty hay when she asked about staying with the animals. He frowned at first and told Maria she should seek out a place in the Mexican quarter on the edge of Magdalena or over in Free Man's Corner a few miles down and off the rail-road tracks, but he eventually agreed when she offered another dollar to sleep in the loft.

Restless, she rose and strapped on her gun belt. She had kept her pistol close at hand while sleeping, just in case the stable owner or one of the hands decided a lone woman—and a Mexican at that—would be an easy target.

Then she stretched before she started down the ladder. She just wanted to use the public jacks behind the main street, but this late at night—or early in the morning—any number of drunk idiots might be wandering around looking for a bit of fun. Or a little trouble. Probably both. The warnings from the angry preacher and Ophelia Barnett swirled in the back of her mind.

On the ground, she passed the horses and mules. Most huffed and stamped the ground as she walked past. As she neared the stable's side door, she heard voices yelling outside and a howl, followed by the deep roar of a shotgun. Maria cracked open the door to look out, trying to determine where the danger was without getting involved.

A monster from a nightmare charged down the street toward her. It stood on two legs like a man, but its body was covered with brown and black fur, and the beast's gaping mouth displayed sharp, pointed teeth. With a growl, it leaped towards her, closing the distance between them in an instant. Maria backpedaled, the door swinging open as she reached for her revolver and fumbled the loop off the hammer. She drew and fired, the shot going wild as the monster crashed into her. Around her, the animals in their stalls began to panic, stamping and kicking, seeking to escape.

The beast bore Maria to the ground, its greater strength and weight too much for her to withstand. The impact on the hard dirt floor of the stable and the weight on her chest forced the breath out of her lungs. Her revolver slipped from her grip and clattered just out of reach. Dazed from hitting her head on the ground, Maria could only put up the weakest of defenses and raised her arms to protect her face and neck from attack.

The beast arched its back, opening its mouth full of razor-sharp teeth. But before it could bite her, the woman in the black dress that she had seen earlier with Ophelia appeared over the monster's shoulder, draping a rosary around its neck. The beast howled in pain, fur and skin smoking where the rosary touched it. The mystery woman pulled the beast off Maria, brought it to its feet, and swung it around, interposing herself between Maria and the monster.

Maria rolled to her revolver and lifted it as Ophelia appeared in the doorway, a glowing silver knife in her hand. Ophelia rushed forward and stabbed the beast. It howled in pain, its thrashing twisting the knife from Ophelia's hand and throwing the mystery woman off its back. She landed near Maria with a grunt of pain. Ophelia swung her double-barreled shotgun around and fired at it point-blank. It flew backward from the impact, its body smoking from the shotgun pellets.

The woman in black sprang to her feet and charged. She stabbed the monster in the chest with the pointed end of the crucifix of her rosary. The creature howled once in agony and collapsed with the woman on top of it, holding the rosary in place. Dead, it changed into a naked man.

"Aw. Just as we thought, he *was* turned on his trip up north." The woman withdrew her bloody rosary and stood. She offered a hand to Maria. "Are you injured? Did it bite you?"

Maria glanced from the dead man to the two women and back again. "No. I'm—it didn't bite me, just knocked me over. I just…"

"I thought I told you to stay under cover, Maria Garcia." Ophelia looked amused.

"What in the name of God was that thing?"

The mystery woman helped Maria to her feet as she answered, "A were-beast. And God played no hand in creating it, Miss Garcia."

"Mrs. Garcia. But please, I'm just Maria."

"I am Elizabeth. A pleasure to meet you, Maria." Elizabeth turned to Ophelia. "I should find the town fathers. I suspect they'll need their nerves settled."

Ophelia nodded. "You reckon we'll get paid, or do you think they'll decide to call us murders and we'll need to run?"

"Since Marshal Greeley and his deputy helped us..."

"At the start, anyway," Ophelia muttered.

Elizabeth nodded in agreement. "At the start. I see no reason we should not be paid." She paused and peered out the stable side door at the crowd gathering. "Saddle the horses just in case." She pointed at Maria. "Is she the one you spoke of?"

"Yup."

Elizabeth smiled tightly at Maria. "Mrs. Garcia, we shall speak in the morning. Assuming, of course, we don't need to flee into the night." She walked out of the stable, walking calmly toward the crowd of townspeople.

Maria stood in stunned silence before Ophelia took her by the arm and led her away from the dead body toward a pair of horses.

Ophelia began saddling the larger of the two animals. "You might want to saddle your own just in case a group of angry locals decide you're with us. Which you are not. But if they get it into their heads to accuse you of a crime, they might toss you in as a bonus since you seem to be suspected of something."

Maria walked up to her horse and gathered its tack. "I—I'm confused."

Ophelia smiled. "Well, Elizabeth and I are in a dangerous line of work. Now, mostly, it's the normal type of bounty hunting, see? Outlaws, thieves, violent men and women. Sometimes it's detective work, finding a person what don't want to be found, recovering a lost valuable. But Elizabeth and I, well, we sometimes take these other jobs."

"Monsters?" After what she'd seen tonight, she decided these two women were exactly what she needed.

"And what do you know about monsters?"

"Enough," Maria replied. "Too much. But you do hunt monsters?"

"Of all kinds, Maria Garcia. You see, Elizabeth has what she calls the gift. She knows when creatures beyond normal understanding threaten folks."

The two women turned at the sound of voices approaching the stable door. Ophelia casually checked her weapons, and Maria reached down and touched the butt of her revolver. She wished she'd taken a moment to reload, but everything happened so fast.

A smiling Elizabeth walked in first, followed by the marshal, his deputy, and a man Maria thought might be the town undertaker. Others followed. They stared down at the body on the floor. Elizabeth approached Ophelia and showed her a leather bag that appeared to be full of coins.

Ophelia turned towards her. "Well, Maria Garcia, I guess we can stop saddling these horses."

FOUR

Maria stood in one corner of the sitting room, watching her companions and the two women they'd thought to hire. Elizabeth sat in a cushioned chair, sipping tea the landlady provided. Charlotte and Anna-Beth sat together on a low couch. Ophelia stood behind Elizabeth, less heavily armed but looking just as dangerous. Ophelia glanced at her, and the tight eyes and slight smile told Maria it was not lost on Ophelia the two of them ended up standing in the wings.

Like servants.

Though Maria doubted Ophelia ever served anyone in her life—at least not willingly—and if she had read last night correctly, Ophelia and Elizabeth were equal partners. Equal partners who'd long since learned how to divide the labor and pass in a white man's world.

Elizabeth sipped her tea and set the cup down on the saucer. In the light of day, Maria found the woman older than she'd first thought, closer to fifty. "First, I feel I must apologize for the landlady's—shall we say—misguided notions."

Maria shrugged. "This isn't first time someone has looked me in the eyes and said my kind isn't welcome in their establishment."

"I reckon not, Maria Garcia." Ophelia's smile grew more lopsided.

"Indeed. Ophelia and I often encounter such treatment. A reason we would be pleased to leave Magdalena soon. Now. I understand you ladies are seeking assistance?"

Charlotte and Anna-Beth shared a long look. Anna-Beth spoke first. "We're going to sound like crazy folk."

Elizabeth waved a dismissive hand at the notion. "I assure you, um..."

"Anna-Beth Carson."

"I assure you, Mrs. Carson, Ophelia and I are well acquainted with what others would call crazy. Please explain."

Charlotte frowned. "Our town..."

Maria sighed in exasperation. Elizabeth wanted the truth. She had seen the monster last night, felt its weight on her body, smelled its rotten breath. Elizabeth deserved the truth. "At least one monster emerged from our local copper mine and set up camp at the pond fed by Millner Creek. Nearly all our menfolk have vanished. First, the miners didn't return, and then the marshal and his deputy disappeared searching for them."

Charlotte sat up straight and spoke next. She pointed at Anne-Beth and Maria. "Anna-Beth's niece went poking around the mine and found tracks heading toward the creek. She came back into town to get help. Mine and Anna-Beth's husbands rode out to scout the creek with some others, including Maria's husband. They vanished as well."

"Finally, well, something came in the night," Maria

said. "The rest of our men, they just walked into the darkness. Like they were sleepwalking."

"All the men?" Ophelia asked.

"A few old men and the young boys didn't seem affected. And we've managed to restrain a handful of the men who tried to walk out of town," Charlotte said.

Elizabeth peered into her teacup and frowned. "So, a Siren? Or something like the Lorelei Rock?"

Maria shrugged. "If you say so. There are stories."

Ophelia snorted. "There are always stories. Besides the niece, did any of you women go investigate further?"

"No," Maria said. "We hired men to try and protect the town, but it either took them or killed them."

"Has anyone seen this beast?" Ophelia stood straight and frowned at Maria.

Anna-Beth and Charlotte both shook their heads.

"After the last group, it sent one back to us. It asked us to join it and called us 'sisters.' That's when I realized that maybe we should seek women hired guns, if we could find them." Maria shifted, uncomfortable under Ophelia's intense gaze.

"How fortunate of you to find us then," Ophelia said. "Tell me, Maria Garcia, why shouldn't we think you're just planning to ambush us once we're in your village and rob us?"

Maria blinked. Her entire body tensed at the accusation. "Why would you think such a thing?"

Elizabeth peered over her cup at Maria. "Because Marshal Greeley here in Magdalena thinks you women are doing just that. So does half this town. I'm guessing one of the first groups to try and help you came from Magdalena?"

"Yes," Maria admitted.

"I'm a bit surprised the good folks of Magdalena

haven't chased you out of town yet. Or just hung you, proof or no of ill deeds." Elizabeth narrowed her eyes. "Are you luring parties of men into the badlands to rob and murder them?"

Maria swallowed. "No."

Elizabeth stood, picked up her rosary from the side table, and offered it to Maria. "Swear it."

Reaching into her side pouch, Maria drew her own rosary, stepped up, and placed it in Elizabeth's hands. With Elizabeth holding both of them, Maria put her hand over Elizabeth's and looked the woman in the eyes. "I swear. Upon my soul, I swear."

Elizabeth smiled and handed back Maria's rosary. "Very well. We will help you. What is the name of your village?"

"You don't even know if we can pay," Charlotte said.

Ophelia grinned. "Can you?"

Anna-Beth fussed with a ribbon on her dress. "Well, yes. It isn't much, but we can pay. We've some money and some silver from the churches and hotel. No one is left to run the smelter, but we can pay you raw copper if you're interested."

"Good enough. Now, Maria Garcia, the name of your village?"

"Tierra de Cobre."

Elizabeth chuckled. "Seriously. Copper Earth?"

Maria laughed. "The founding fathers lacked imagination."

"ARE YOU SURE?" Ophelia asked. She sat on the windowsill in Elizabeth's room at the boarding house. Ophelia shared it as well, but the less the landlady knew about that, the better. Ophelia would walk out under the watchful eyes of Mrs. Durger and would sneak back in like a damned thief to be with her beloved.

Elizabeth sat in a low chair, braiding her hair. The New Mexico Territory heat bothered Elizabeth more than she'd ever admit to Ophelia, and getting her spill of hair under control would help keep her neck cool. Elizabeth wearing her hair bound was fine with Ophelia. She loved running her fingers through Elizabeth's long blonde locks but damned if it didn't find its way in your nose and mouth if she left it loose while sleeping or making love.

"Yes," Elizabeth said. "I felt it when Maria swore. They need us. And we will need help."

"And they can pay. I'd just rather work a nice, normal job though. How are we going to find help, Beth? I refuse to count on the town's women. A few might be steady, but if you're right—"

"And you know I am."

"This will be beyond their worst nightmare. We're going to need professionals." Movement caught Ophelia's eye. A young woman dressed more for an evening out to the theater back east, not the dusty streets of a small territorial county seat, walked straight toward the boarding house. "Shit."

Elizabeth paused her movements. "What?"

Ophelia sighed. "She's found us again."

"We have our first."

"Are you kidding? I said professionals, not soft little Philadelphia ladies playing at reporter."

Elizabeth finished her braid and tied it off at the end with a bit of black ribbon. "If Miss Clara Dashelle is desperate to write her story, why should we disappoint her?"

"Is this one of your flashes of insight?"

"If I say yes, will it make you feel better?"

"No." Ophelia waved out the window as Clara smiled up at her.

The sounds of indistinct voices drifted up the stairs, slowly drawing nearer. At a nod from Elizabeth, Ophelia moved toward the door. Elizabeth grinned. "You might as well let her in." Ophelia opened the door, and their unexpected guest reached the top of the landing.

Clara smiled at Ophelia. "Ophelia! What a pleasure to see you!"

"Miss Dashelle," Ophelia replied, stepping aside to allow the woman entry.

Clara flounced into the room and settled on the wooden stool. "Ladies, I understand you both dealt with another creature of darkness last night. I'm sorry I'm too late to witness you dispatch the fiend." She produced a pencil and notepad from her handbag. "I'd love to hear the entire story!"

Elizabeth settled back into the armchair and leaned forward. "Suppose, Ms. Dashelle, instead of recounting our story after the fact, we offer you the opportunity to report in the field?"

Clara blinked. "Are you suggesting what I believe you are suggesting?"

"Sadly, yes," Ophelia sighed.

"Oh! I'd be thrilled!"

"We need something from you in return," Elizabeth said.

"Of course!"

Elizabeth leaned back in the chair. "I know you have contacts and know other women like us."

Clara bit her bottom lip and shifted in the chair. "Yes. A—a few."

"We need to assemble a crew for our next mission and

we need to do it quickly. In exchange for helping, you will ride with us, helping as you might and reporting as you wish."

"You're serious? Swear you won't use me for these contacts to leave me behind if the opportunity presents itself?"

Elizabeth gave her a long look before picking up her rosary. Ophelia considered intervening. She didn't want the greenhorn from Philadelphia slowing them, didn't want to babysit the young woman. Once Elizabeth swore on the rosary, there would be no going back. But even though she wanted to intervene, she didn't. She would have to trust her partner's intuition on this one.

"This I swear to you, Clara Dashelle. You are a part of this now, may the Lord protect you."

"And the mission? What can you tell me? You know, so I can explain in my telegraphs."

"A town nearby needs protecting, and those protectors must be women. And there is pay. Once a few interested parties arrive, our employer can explain more."

Ophelia sat on the edge of the bed and caught Clara's eyes. "But rest assured, there are monsters to fight. There will be blood and possible death, Miss Dashelle. Your safety is not guaranteed."

Clara took a deep breath, whether to steady her nerves or calm her excitement, Ophelia couldn't tell. "Yes. I agree. I'll go send a few messages. I can think of a couple of women who could be here in a week or less," Clara said. "Ladies." Clara smiled at Elizabeth and Ophelia. "This is so exciting!" she said before she exited the room.

Ophelia moved to watch the woman's retreating form out the window as Elizabeth stood and stretched. "She's going to get her fool-self killed chasing after us."

"Perhaps. It is not given to most souls to know the date

of their meeting with the Lord, so why worry? Do you think we'll be safe here for a few days more, my love?"

"I think so, but I'll go ahead and make arrangements to move us out to Free Men's Corner just in case, though I doubt Miss Dashelle or our clients will be comfortable there."

"Discomfort will be good for them," Elizabeth said.

"Uh-huh. Doubt the folks in Free Man's will be pleased with them either, but I can make it right." She paused with her hand on the door. "Liz, this one feels off to me."

"Yes. I feel it, too. Let's see who our new partner finds for us. Perhaps that will tip the feeling to something more positive."

Elizabeth moved into her and kissed her with soft passion.

"I need to go secure our bolt hole," Ophelia said. "Stay out of trouble while I'm away, please?"

"I'll do my best."

CHAPTER

FIVE

Abigail Long watched out the window as the train rolled down the rails, carrying her to her destination. She allowed the rails' rhythm and the car's swaying to soothe her. Soon enough, she would be immersed in whatever trouble Miss Clara Dashelle had summoned her toward. Abigail might have ignored the telegraph that arrived by Western Union to her spartan hotel room in Ft. Collins, but the emphasis Clara had placed on how the job could only be handled by a woman intrigued her. She chuckled softly to herself. She was probably reading too much into the telegraph.

Abigail reached into her bag for the book she'd been reading. She had brought the bare minimum since Clara explained that time was urgent. Abigail sold her horse and most of her gear, figuring she'd replace them when she arrived, and took the faster trains, first to Santa Fe and then to Magdalena.

Ignoring the disapproving frowns directed at her by the passing conductor, she opened the battered copy of Jane Austen's novel *Emma*. She had picked it up in Ft. Collins in the same trading post where she'd sold off her belongings, pleased to find something worth reading on the long ride. Adjusting her seat, she opened the book, ready to immerse herself in other people's problems, in this case, the title character's well-meaning but misguided actions.

"Hello, Abigail."

With an internal sigh, Abigail carefully placed the cloth bookmark and closed the novel. If it had been a male voice saying her name, she would have been instantly alert and ready for trouble. But this was a woman's voice and one she recognized by the accent, though she was not entirely sure where in Eastern Europe the speaker hailed from. Abigail looked up and smiled at the small woman standing over her. A yellow and blue scarf covered her black hair, and she wore a plain blouse, skirt, and boots and carried a small bag. Her face was thin and striking, her eyes bright blue, and she looked like a stiff wind would knock her over.

"Sofia. Dare I ask what brings you here?"

"Trouble. I suspect the same trouble you walk towards. I overheard the conductors gossiping about a woman brazenly wearing men's clothes and carrying a revolver for all to see. I thought it might be you. When I spotted you reading, I knew this was the correct place."

"Are you following me?"

"No." Sofia glanced at the empty spot next to Abigail. "May I?"

"My apologies. Yes, please join me."

Sofia settled right next to her, so close their legs touched, and peered directly into Abigail's eyes. "You are heading to Magdalena. You have received a telegraph about a town that needs assistance, and that assistance can only be women."

"Seen the future, have you?"

Sofia laughed and leaned back. "No. I, too, am

summoned to Magdalena for this purpose. Your being on the train makes sense. They have requested both an expert gun and a master of mystical arts."

"Master of mystical arts, are we now?"

Sofia smiled. "You doubt?"

Abigail raised a hand in surrender. "I've worked with you enough times to understand magic is real, but when last we parted, you were using parlor tricks to befuddle dance hall drunks."

"No need to work harder than necessary. A little song and dance, a little sleight-of-hand, a quick tumble with the dark exotic stranger, and they part with their coins easily and happily. Real magic is not needed for such men."

"And they get stupid for the accent."

"So stupid," Sofia agreed. "But you, my friend, have become the hero of dime novels and darling of newspaper columns these days. Your exploits are nearly mythical."

Abigail frowned. "Spare me from writers and reporters."

Sofia laughed. "I should not tease you…"

"Please don't."

"Then I will not. It is good to see you, Abigail."

"The same. And if this little job needs a 'Master of Mystical Arts,' I'm glad it is you." Abigail turned to face Sofia. "Now, it seems you know all about my travels, so tell me what you've been doing since we parted ways in Abilene."

FUMBLING to open her pocket watch with her free hand, Abigail checked the time. They should be arriving in Magdalena in a few minutes. She supposed she should wake Sofia from her nap.

Once the two women caught up on the three years of their lives, they had settled into companionable silence, Abigail reading her novel, Sofia studying from a bundle of loose papers she had unrolled onto her lap, frowning and making occasional wordless exclamations. After nearly an hour, Sofia rolled up the papers, tied them with a bit of red string, returned them to her bag, and snuggled into Abigail. Abigail found her arm draped protectively around Sofia as the woman murmured in her sleep. The passing conductor frowned at them as he walked his rounds, but Abigail didn't care what the man thought.

I should wake her. Abigail gave Sofia a little squeeze. "Sofia."

Sofia jerked awake, bolting up and out of Abigail's embrace, eyes wild. "No! Run! It will…" She paused and blinked. "Oh. I was asleep." She sat back on the bench beside Abigail, right on the edge. "I'm sorry if I startled you."

"It's fine. Nightmare?"

"I pray it is just a nightmare and not a vision." The train began to slow, the floor under them vibrating as the brakes started to engage. "Have we arrived?"

Abigail nodded. "Yes. That's why I woke you."

"Then let us prepare to meet our destiny."

The train huffed to a stop at the small train station on the outskirts of Magdalena. Abigail and Sofia gathered their belongings. A handful of people exited the passenger car ahead of them, chatting and cheerful in the bright light of day.

"I have a bag I'll need to retrieve," Sofia said.

"I'll come with you."

Abigail adjusted her leather gloves, checked her Smith and Wesson Russian, and adjusted the strap of the leather bag hanging over her shoulder. She stepped down from the train and waved off the station agent who moved to help with her small Gladstone.

She watched as Sofia spoke with a train porter. He disappeared, then reappeared with a surprisingly large bag.

Abigail strolled over to help. "I can carry it if you can handle mine."

Sofia smiled. "I have made arrangements to have it delivered to the hotel." She drew a small pouch from her belt, opened it, pulled out a shiny coin, and handed it to the porter. "I think there is only one hotel in the town." She smiled at Abigail. "Shall we?"

Abigail shook her head in amusement. She turned to the town, a hundred yards from the station. They walked down from the platform and toward the local hotel to meet these people who needed help in the form of a hired gun and a sorceress.

Ophelia glanced around the hotel's lobby, taking stock of her surroundings. Elizabeth and Clara sat on the long couch. On the low wooden table before them rested a tea service the hotel keeper's wife had brought out. The hotel keeper, a man in his late twenties, stood behind the counter, a dozen keys on pegs behind him. A girl swept the floor. A pair of old men sat at a round table, reading news-papers. Clara checked her pocket watch and the movement drew Ophelia's attention.

"She should be here anytime," Clara said. "She telegraphed she'd be on the 3:10 from Santa Fe."

Elizabeth glanced at Clara. "You seem nervous."

"Do you know Abigail Long?"

"I only know her by reputation. Including your piece on her dealing with the Billings boys."

"She is…intense."

The hotel doors opened, and in walked a woman in men's clothing, clean and dapper, with a small string tie. A Smith and Wesson revolver rested in its holster at her hip. She wore leather gloves. A second woman followed her, tall and thin, dressed like someone's farm wife. She carried a small handbag.

The first woman glanced around the hotel lobby before setting her bag on the floor, shrugging the shoulder bag off, and taking off her hat. She nodded to the man behind the counter and turned to approach Clara and Elizabeth. Ophelia didn't know her but recognized her as another dangerous woman living in a man's world.

Elizabeth and Clara stood. Clara smiled. "Abigail!"

Abigail reached out a hand. "Miss Dashelle. A pleasure to see you again." They shook, and she offered her hand to Elizabeth next. "My name is Abigail Long." She waved at the second woman. "And this is my friend Sofia, who I believe is here on the same business as I am."

Elizabeth stared hard at Sofia for several moments. The look the two women exchanged reminded Ophelia of her exchange with Abigail, measuring each other. Finally, Elizabeth nodded to the woman and reached out to shake her hand. "Welcome."

Sofia took Elizabeth's hand. The two women held eye contact for a heartbeat, still obviously trying to sort something out. "Thank you. I am Sofia Podany. From El Paso of late, but previously of Boston."

Clara smiled. "Oh! I've friends in Boston! Are you related to the Podanys of Back Bay?"

"No."

"Oh." Clara deflated and sank back onto the couch. "Well, charmed to meet you."

Ophelia sighed quietly. She would need to keep her

annoyance with Clara in check. It wasn't as if the woman had done injury to her or Elizabeth. Clara just kept tracking them down and trying to, as Clara once said, "Document your adventures." Ophelia didn't care for the attention from newspapers or dime novels. Their job was hard enough without a reputation for weirdness following them around. She turned her attention back to the conversation.

Elizabeth shook Abigail's hand next. "I am Elizabeth. You know Ms. Dashelle. The lady behind us watching you suspiciously is my partner, Ophelia Barnett, and yes, my client is hiring for a job requiring women who can fight." Elizabeth waved at the chairs across the table from the couch.

Ophelia noticed the watchful gaze of the hotel keeper standing behind his counter as the group resettled. She frowned as the man leaned down and whispered something into the ear of the girl sweeping the floor. The girl handed him the broom and ran off behind the counter and out of sight.

Abigail Long waited until Sofia and Elizabeth sat down before she perched on the edge of a wooden chair like a hawk ready to take flight at a moment's notice.

"Before we go any further," Abigail said, "I need to know a few things. Where is your client? Why do they specifically need women who are handy in a fight to, I am assuming, defend their town?"

Ophelia settled into a watchful silence as Elizabeth explained. *This should be interesting,* she thought.

"The clients are the people of Tierra de Cobre. Their representatives are here in town and should join us shortly. As for why they need us..." Elizabeth leaned forward and lowered her voice. "At least one beast of unknown origins has emerged from their copper mine and has taken up residence near a local pond."

"It has taken most of their men," Clara added, a bit too loud for Ophelia's taste.

Abigail frowned at the two women. "Beast? Taken? What nonsense is this?"

Sofia leaned toward Elizabeth, a small smile on her lips. "My dear friend Abigail, despite having seen magic with her own eyes, still refuses to believe in certain parts of the mystical world," she said softly.

"I've seen you work magic, so I know it's real," Abigail replied. "Just because magic is real doesn't mean these mythical monsters are."

"Oh. You are a sorceress?" Clara asked.

Sofia turned her gaze to Clara. "Yes. My mentors sent me. You telegraphed them seeking assistance with a matter involving supernatural forces."

Clara instantly brightened. "Ah! The Fox sisters? They replied they'd sent help."

"I am that help." Sofia turned her gaze to Abigail. "I can assure you monsters from your darkest nightmares are real. Please trust me on this and keep an open mind." Sofia's smile widened. "Also, it is a paying job."

Elizabeth took a sip of tea and glanced from Abigail to Sofia. "You two have worked together before?"

Abigail nodded. "Sofia and I go back a bit."

"Most recently, we dealt with a cursed puzzle box," Sofia replied. "She understands cursed objects but won't believe in monsters like Wendigo or vampires."

"I've seen a cursed puzzle box," Abigail countered.

"Company," Ophelia said.

Everyone turned toward the hotel's front door as it opened. Maria entered. Everyone stood, and Elizabeth motioned her over. "I should introduce you to our employer. Abigail Long, Sofia Podany, this is Maria Garcia, one of the women from Tierra de Cobre."

Abigail nodded. "Miss."

"Missus, but Maria is fine." Maria turned to Elizabeth. "Are they…?"

"Yes," Elizabeth said.

Clara stood with a broad smile as she walked to Maria and offered her hand. "Clara Dashelle, from Philadelphia. I'm so pleased to meet you, Mrs. Garcia."

"Maria. Please, just Maria."

"Well, Mrs. Garcia, I only need one question answered," Abigail said. "Can you meet my price?"

"What price?" Maria asked. Ophelia noticed the young woman had started to look overwhelmed by all the attention.

"I want a warm bed. Three hot meals a day. A quiet place to sleep. For as long as I want to stay. A horse and tack when I'm ready to move on."

"Yes. Yes. We can give you this. And the rest of you? Miss Dashelle?"

"Oh. Well! I'm here for Elizabeth and Ophelia," she said. "This is my chance to chronicle their story as it happens!"

"As for me," Sofia said, "I swear I will ask for nothing your village will not be pleased to part with."

Ophelia shook her head. "You're all insane. Cash. Or silver. Or gold. Hell, even enough raw copper would be fine."

"And of course, the destruction of your monster," Elizabeth said.

Maria settled her eyes on Elizabeth. "I agree with Ophelia. You are all insane. But so am I. Thank you."

"How far away is your town, Maria?" Abigail asked.

"Two days, three if you're moving slow."

Abigail turned to Clara. "Are we expecting any more recipients of your telegraphs to arrive?"

"No," Clara replied with a shake of her head. "Two never responded, and I've been informed the other woman I tried to contact recently passed."

"Well, as we are all in agreement, I suggest we all get a decent day's rest and night's sleep before we ride out," Ophelia said.

"I'll need a horse and to replace most of my gear," Abigail said. "I would suspect a town this size has a stable, possibly with horses to sell or rent?"

"We are going to need horses for the three of you," Ophelia said. "Elizabeth and I have our own, and I saw Maria and her group ride in."

Abigail nodded. "So, mounts for myself, Sofia, and Miss Dashelle. Might be smarter to try and rent them from the stable."

"If they have them," Sofia said.

"And if they'll rent to anyone going to Tierra de Cobre," Maria added.

"Oh?" Abigail asked. "Will there be a problem?"

Maria was saved from answering as the hotel door opened. Ophelia came to wary attention as Marshal Greeley and his deputy entered, both men holding rifles. Abigail stood and took a similar posture.

Elizabeth rose and stepped forward. "Marshal. Is there an issue?"

Greeley shuffled his feet. "Look, Miss Elizabeth, we appreciate all you've done for us."

"Thank you."

"But some folks are uneasy with you and your friend." He looked at Ophelia and back to Elizabeth.

"Ah." Elizabeth gave him a knowing smile and a nod

of her head. "You want to know when we will be leaving fair Magdalena, I take it?"

"Yes, ma'am. I don't want to seem ungrateful, but yes." He turned his attention to Maria. "Same question for you and your friends from Tierra de Cobre, miss."

Maria stood. "Maria Garcia. We'll be riding out first thing tomorrow for Tierra de Cobre. The next day at the latest."

"Yes," Elizabeth said. "As will Ophelia and I."

Marshal Greeley studied Elizabeth for a few seconds and frowned. "I would consider our earlier conversation more carefully, Miss Elizabeth."

"I have. We ride for Tierra de Cobre in the morning, Marshal, with Mrs. Garcia as our guide."

"On your head." Marshal Greeley turned to Abigail. "Abigail Long. I want to see you riding out with them or back on the train to Santa Fe."

"I plan to ride to this Tierra de Cobre."

"I just want you to know Jack Billings rode into town about an hour ago. I know you have a history with his kin. I doubt he knows you're here, but I'd appreciate it if any trouble between you two didn't land in Magdalena."

Abigail nodded. "I will do my best, but I will not run from him if attacked."

"I understand. Just try not to cross paths with him." With a last look at the entire group, Marshal Greeley and his deputy warily backed out the door.

Ophelia felt the group relax a bit as the two lawmen exited. They finally all sat down again, Abigail last and only after she shifted her chair to keep an eye on the front door. Ophelia was a little surprised it took the woman this long to make the move.

"Please," Sofia said, "explain why the good lawman

doesn't want you traveling to this Tierra de Cobre, Miss Elizabeth."

Elizabeth sighed and turned to the hotel keeper. "If the kitchen would be so kind as to bring us a pot of tea and more cups, please."

~

OPHELIA SNUGGLED DOWN with Elizabeth on the narrow bed in Elizabeth's room. They'd both changed into their sleeping clothes, though Ophelia kept her weapons near to hand on the bedpost. It felt good to lie here with her love and steal these quiet moments when they could. Ophelia would need to sneak back out before the landlady awoke in the morning and reenter through the back door. But that was a problem for later. "So…she's a witch?" Ophelia took up the thread of a previous conversation.

"A sorcerer," Elizabeth said. "Sofia's powers are learned. They come from books and scrolls and hidden knowledge, not drawn from nature."

"Or faith?

"Or faith."

Ophelia shifted in the bed. "Well, I'm glad you've retained enough faith to work your magic. I'm also glad you set those silly restrictions on loving aside."

"There are excellent reasons for one to be celibate."

"If you say so." Ophelia finally gave voice to what she'd been thinking. "Beth, it still feels off."

"Yes. We're one short, I think. But we will find them, and I will understand better."

"Please, God, let her be a fighter."

Elizabeth rolled over to face her. "You're too concerned with guns. You and Abigail Long will be quite formidable in battle. I suspect Mrs. Garcia of depths of nerve not yet mined. As for Miss Dashelle, we shall understand her part before long."

Ophelia tried and could not hide her annoyance with Clara Dashelle. "Well, I would be happy to leave her behind, but if you say we need her…"

"And we do."

"Then that's good enough for me."

Elizabeth smiled at her and pushed Ophelia onto her back. She did not resist. "You are entirely too tense. I think it is time to remind you why I set aside my vows and my past."

"Well, if you insist." Ophelia gave herself over to the moment as Elizabeth kissed along her neck and jaw, kissed her lips, climbed on top of her, and kissed downward, vanishing under the covers as Ophelia shifted and gasped. "Yes. Right there."

CHAPTER
SIX

Maria stood in the street before Anna-Beth's cousin's home and Elizabeth and Clara waited with her. Neither Anna-Beth nor Charlotte came to the hotel to meet with the mercenaries they planned to hire. When Maria tried to find out why they hadn't come, Anna-Beth's cousin's husband had stood in the open door screaming at Maria to "get her goddamned Mexican ass" off his property or else he'd make sure she never bothered anyone again.

After relating the story to the others, Elizabeth decided she and Maria would go to the house together. Clara, her reporter's instincts for drama sensing a story, decided to join them. Anna-Beth and Charlotte slipped out of the house as they reached the front gate. Anna-Beth looked over her shoulder at the door behind her, nervous. Charlotte's lips tightened.

"What?" Maria asked. "What happened?"

Anna-Beth shifted her weight from one foot to the other and back again. "I—I'm not coming back with you. I'm staying here in Magdalena. I can't go back. I can't."

Maria glanced at Charlotte. She had half-expected Anna-Beth to wilt, but not Charlotte. "And you? Are you staying behind as well?"

"Yes. I'm sorry. It's safe here, and I'm not going back. I'll try to sell the printing press and move out to California. I've family there."

Elizabeth cleared her throat. "Do you intend to set aside your lives and abandon your homes and claims?"

Charlotte frowned but nodded firmly. "There's nothing left there for me. I don't want to run my dead husband's newspaper."

Clara sidled up to Charlotte, holding out a small card. "Excuse me? Not to be crass, but I would be extremely interested in purchasing your press."

Charlotte took the card. "If Tierra de Cobre doesn't kill you, you can wire me whatever you're comfortable paying. I'll contact you when I reach Sacramento."

"I hate to see you throw everything away," Maria said.

"Better to throw those things away than to throw away our lives." Anna-Beth's agitation increased. "Can you let Daisy know? Tell her she should come to Magdalena, and I'll see to her future."

Maria nodded. "I will speak with her."

"And Maria, we think you should leave the horses and mule. Except for your horse."

Maria's whole body tightened. "They're not our horses or mule, so no, I will not be leaving them. They return to the stable in Tierra de Cobre with me."

"Maria. Please understand," Anna-Beth pled. "That town, I don't think it can be saved. Whatever came out of the mine, it can't be stopped. Fetch Daisy and come back here. I'll help you find work."

"And when the beast that escaped the mine finishes

with your town, do you think Magdalena will still be safe?" Elizabeth asked.

"I—I don't know," Anna-Beth admitted.

"But it is someone else's problem," Charlotte said firmly. "The army or someone. I don't know who, but I am not throwing my life away fighting that…whatever the hell it is. I'm done. I'm off for California, and if it finds me there…" Charlotte shrugged. "Then I guess the end of the world preachers are right."

Looking from one woman to the other, Maria felt the keen sting of abandonment. She decided arguing would be useless. "If this is your decision, I've nothing left to say to you. Stay here. Hide. But I am going home. Good luck to you both. Goodbye."

She turned and left the two women standing in front of the house and walked back into town proper. After a few moments, Elizabeth and Clara followed.

MARIA APPROACHED the stable as Abigail, Ophelia, Elizabeth, Clara, and Sofia waited with the horses. They quickly loaded the mule with most of everyone's baggage, with Clara paying particular attention to a small crate nestled in among the bags. The group appeared ready to ride, though Maria noted Clara's riding dress looked new. *Well, it will get dusty soon enough.*

"I heard about your friends, Maria Garcia." Ophelia frowned at her.

"Since the others are not coming, I will need a few minutes to saddle their horses."

Abigail nodded to her. "We've taken the liberty, ma'am."

Maria noted the two horses, saddled and ready to ride. "Well, I guess we need to hire two fewer horses."

"Think we could cut a half day off if we kept all the horses and switched out periodically? I'm willing to pay the extra," Abigail said.

Ophelia chuckled. "If you're paying, I figure the extra horses might be useful."

"Abigail Long!" a voice cried out. Maria looked down the street. A white man who looked like any cowhand walked briskly toward them.

Maria heard Abigail sigh as she turned to face the man.

"I'm guessing that's Jack Billings," Ophelia said.

The man marched up to Abigail, menace in his eyes. "I've been looking for you, Abigail Long."

Maria reached down and casually took the loop off the hammer of her Colt. She silently prayed it didn't come to violence, but wanted to be ready if things went sour.

"I know," Abigail replied. "I'm sorry about your cousins, but they made their choices. You don't have to make the same ones. I gave them a fair chance to walk away. I'm willing to give you that chance as well." Abigail stepped out from the group of women into the street, keeping her opponent in sight. "I am telling you, sir, do not cross me."

Ophelia stepped up next to Maria. "The fool. He doesn't understand what's going to happen if he pushes her. He can't see it."

"They going to fight?" Clara asked.

"Yes," Ophelia said.

"We should be ready to ride," Elizabeth said. "Not getting pulled into nonsense like this."

Maria stood in horrified fascination as Abigail and Jack Billings faced each other.

"Should we fetch the Marshal?" Clara asked.

Abigail stepped closer to Billings. "I suspect Marshal Greeley will be here in short order."

Billings narrowed his eyes. "This is none of the Marshal's business. This is just about you and me."

Maria watched Ophelia slowly draw her shotgun from behind her back. Jack Billings would be caught in a crossfire if it came to violence. She noticed Elizabeth and Sofia steer Clara clear of the two potential combatants from the corner of her eye. She glanced up the street to see Marshal Greeley leave his office.

Abigail held firm in the face of the man's anger. "I have no quarrel with you, sir."

Marshal Greeley pushed his way past the gathered onlookers. "Jack Billings, you just stop right there."

"No!" Billings shouted. As Marshal Greeley reached to restrain him, Billings pushed the marshal hard to the ground. He turned on Abigail.

In a sudden burst of movement, both parties reached for their weapons. Abigail drew and fired twice into Jack Billings's chest before his pistol cleared his leather holster. Abigail fired a third time. Finishing his draw, Billings blinked in confusion and fired one round into the ground before dropping his revolver and falling face down in the dirt. On the street, people emerged from businesses and homes to see the aftermath.

Abigail looked to Marshal Greeley. "Are you injured?"

"Just my pride." The Marshal stood and looked down at Billings's body. "Damned fool."

Abigail reloaded her pistol. "I'm sorry, sir. I tried."

"I saw the whole thing. Just…get on your horse and leave my town before anything else happens."

"Yes, sir." Abigail climbed onto her waiting horse, Maria holding the reins.

"I'm sorry you witnessed such violence, ma'am," Abigail said.

"Just call me Maria, and we should ride before the marshal changes his mind."

"Agreed," Ophelia said. She steered a stunned Clara to her horse and helped her mount.

The women rode fast out of town as Marshal Greeley and other locals stood over the dead man in the street.

CHAPTER

SEVEN

Ophelia kept a careful eye on her surroundings and the other women, whom she considered her charges, women to keep alive until they revealed their usefulness to the mission.

Except Elizabeth and Abigail. She'd been with Elizabeth long enough to know her love's worth in a tight spot. Abigail paid keen attention to the badlands they rode and Ophelia knew she could handle herself if there was trouble. So she studied the others instead. Maria and Clara rode side-by-side, chatting, though Maria kept a wary eye on their surroundings. Sofia rode in the middle of the pack, nose down in a book as they rode along. At a signal from Abigail, Ophelia took point while Abigail dropped back and minded the rear, swapping positions. After a few minutes, Ophelia paused, letting the others catch up. She rode close to Elizabeth. "We've picked up a shadow."

"Oh?" Elizabeth didn't seem particularly surprised.

"Yeah. About five miles out of Magdalena."

"Trouble?"

"I always expect trouble."

Abigail trotted her horse up to them. "Should one of us chat with the young woman trailing us?" Abigail asked.

Ophelia nodded. "I figured to do just that."

"Do you want backup?"

Ophelia smiled. "Honestly? I'd rather you stay and protect the other womenfolk."

Elizabeth snorted and laughed, drawing the attention of the others.

"Is something funny?" Sofia asked, looking up from her book.

Ophelia waved her off, and Sofia shrugged and returned to reading, trusting her horse to carry her safely.

"It will be dark in a couple of hours. Let's set up camp over there." Abigail pointed at a spot just ahead.

Ophelia looked at it carefully, then nodded in agreement. "Good sight lines, near a spring, but not on it. I like it."

Ophelia called a stop, and the group set up camp for the evening. Maria and Abigail moved with confidence, Ophelia noted. Clara struggled to set up her bedroll and assist the others. *At least she asks questions and she's trying to be helpful.* Once they prepared food and tended the horses, Ophelia gave Elizabeth a look and walked away from the rest, vanishing into the gathering darkness.

Ophelia moved sure-footed, carrying only her revolver and knives. She slowly climbed a slight rise in the ground thirty yards from the camp and slunk silently around a set of low shrubs. At last, she came to a spot where it was clear that someone had knelt to observe the camp below before moving away.

She started to turn to follow the tracks. There was a noise behind her, and Ophelia froze. "You pull that trigger, and a whole world of pain is going to fall on your head." Ophelia stood slowly, hands up, and turned to face a young native woman aiming a battered Springfield rifle at her. "If you'd be willing to talk, we might be able to reach an accord. Do you need food? Water?"

The woman scowled. "I need nothing from you."

Ophelia nodded. "Okay. I'm just wondering why you've been following us. It seems a bit unfriendly-like. Makes a person think you might be planning to try to kill us all in our sleep and steal our horses."

"I am no horse thief!"

Ophelia smiled and raised an eyebrow.

The young woman shrugged. "Well, I steal horses from the white soldiers. But that is different."

Silent as a ghost, Elizabeth emerged from the shadows, the weak light of the moon glinting on her silver crucifix. "Of course, it is different, my child. Now, I would be thankful if you'd stop pointing your weapon at my partner Please gather your belongings and join us for our meal."

The woman stared at Elizabeth for several heartbeats before lowering her rifle. "I will join you, *Shik'isn.*"

OPHELIA ATE her dinner slowly and carefully. Most of the women sat near the fire eating or, in Clara's case, scribbling away in her notebook by the dying light of the cooking fire. Maria and Abigail stood off to one side, Maria looking into the darkness, Abigail keeping an eye on the young woman they had brought back to camp. Ophelia pointed with her knife between the native woman and Sofia. "Now, help me understand the relationship here since you two seem to know each other."

Sofia nodded. "Yes. Ha-o..."

The woman frowned and cut off Sofia mid-sentence. "No. That child died. I am simply Kira now."

"And you are from these lands?" Elizabeth asked.

"I am of the *Haisndayin.*"

Ophelia leaned over to Clara. "Jicarilla Apache," she said softly.

Sofia reached out and touched Kira's arm. "I am pleased to see you again." Sofia turned back to her meal. "Kira and I once worked together in El Paso."

"We were whores."

"Oh!" Clara blushed in surprise.

Sofia gave Clara a tight smile. "One does what one must to survive, though I was not a whore. I was a—show-girl—a courtesan. I only took gentlemen clients if I wished."

"Fancy whore," Kira laughed.

Sofia smiled at the younger woman. "Well, I'm pleased to see you again and happy you escaped."

Kira pushed her skirt around to reveal the hilt of a large knife. "Cut my way out." The knife disappeared back into Kira's clothing.

"I am not surprised." Sofia paused. "I should have helped you when I left. I knew your situation was different from the other girls. I left you behind. I am sorry."

"Escape?" Clara asked. "I mean, I know…ladies such as yourselves…as you were…are sometimes under the control of a whoremonger or house madam, but something in the way you said 'escape' seems even more sinister than normal."

Ophelia answered. "Sometimes young native women, most of them little more than children, are taken and sold."

"But…" Clara paused.

Ophelia gave her a tight smile. "Officially, slavery is ended in these here United States, but if your skin is of a darker shade, well, maybe in certain places, them laws don't get enforced."

Kira nodded. "Plenty of men paid good money to bed me. I helped myself to some coin when I left."

"Oh," Clara said. "Well, I am happy that you are with us now."

Elizabeth cleared her throat. "If I may ask, why were you tracking us if not for food or robbery?"

Ophelia leaned toward Clara and whispered, "Though she's happily eating our dinner."

Kira gestured at Maria and said, "When I saw her riding back to Tierra de Cobre, I understood my path was your path."

Clara peered up from her notebook. "I'd think you would return to your home and family once you'd escaped your…situation."

Kira shrugged. "Most of them are dead or fled to the mountains in the north. Those remaining would not want me."

"You say your path is our path because we travel back to Tierra de Cobre," Elizabeth said. "Do you know what is happening there?"

"I will not speak of it in the darkness. Not under the moon. I will speak of it when the sun shines high tomorrow to drive away the shadows."

Sofia leaned forward. "You know what lurks at the creek?"

"Yes. I fear the miners set a thing my people fear free." Kira finished her food. She stood and gathered her small bundle of possessions and rifle and moved off from the camp. She paused at the edge of the firelight. "I will sleep here. In the morning, I will hunt for us."

Ophelia glanced at Clara again. "Probably going to kill

a couple of those big Chuckwalla lizards. Damned tasty if cooked right."

"Um…lizards?"

Elizabeth laughed. "They taste exactly like chicken, Miss Dashelle."

~

MARIA PEERED INTO THE DARKNESS, the campfire behind her. She could hear the conversation, and she knew Abigail stood nearby. *Probably worried I might wander off into the night. As if I wasn't raised out here.*

"Mrs. Garcia."

Maria turned to face Abigail. "Maria."

"Maria. How are you handling all," Abigail waved a hand at nothing in particular, "this?"

"My town is under siege. A monster lurks in the shadows. My only means of making a living is useless as things stand. My friends have abandoned me, and my husband is likely dead or worse. I may well be dead in the next few days. I would say I'm handling things well."

"You don't need to fight. Fighting is why you hired us."

"Yes, I do."

Abigail pointed at the gun on Maria's hip. "I see you wear a Colt."

"My husband's. Well, his backup pistol. He never felt comfortable with it, I think."

"And your husband?"

Maria stepped closer to Abigail and gave the camp a quick look. "The beast took him early. I've seen what it does to men. He is dead."

"I am sorry."

"Thank you."

They stood in silence for a few moments until Abigail

nodded to Maria's weapon. "Do you know how to use it? Can you kill, Mrs. Garcia?"

"Yes. I can use this and I think I can kill. Please don't treat me as if I'm some foolish child. I will fight."

"I can only imagine what you're going through," Abigail said. "Though I admit to being a bit skeptical concerning the monster thing."

Maria frowned. "You'll understand soon enough."

"Well, Maria, if you are dead set on fighting for your home, I plan to see to it you and anyone willing to fight possess the skills needed. When we reach your town, I will start teaching you shooting. Good night, Maria."

"Good night, Miss Long."

"Abigail."

"Abigail. Good night."

EIGHT

Elizabeth studied the various plants Kira added to their morning meal. She wasn't familiar with many of them, but Kira appeared competent and confident in cooking the meal, and she didn't believe the young woman planned to poison them. She also returned with three jackrabbits, welcome fresh meat and a pleasant change from eating pemmican and hard tack. Or beans. Elizabeth was tired of eating beans all the time in small-town hotels and stagecoach stations. She'd bought a little hard cheese in Magdalena for the trip and Ophelia brewed a strong pot of coffee to warm everyone. The women chatted as they ate their breakfast.

"But if you don't have a rail station, how do you receive mail and supplies?" Clara asked Maria.

Maria paused with a bit of cheese in her hand. "Supplies come by train to Magdalena and are brought out by wagon. We ship copper back the same way."

Sofia gave Maria a curious look. "Do you fear the good folk of Magdalena might cut off your supplies? They seem pretty angry with Tierra de Cobre."

Swallowing her food, Maria frowned. "I'm not sure what we'd do. I suppose we should consider it. The supply wagon and the mail hack haven't come in over a month. I've picked up mail for the whole town, or what's left of it."

"You will persevere and continue with life," Elizabeth said. Ophelia settled next to her with coffee and food. "Which is all anyone can do."

"True enough," Ophelia agreed. She pointed at Clara with her eating knife. "Last chance to turn back, Miss Dashelle. You could make it to Magdalena by nightfall."

Clara smiled. She looked rougher after a day's ride and a night sleeping on the ground but undeterred. "You'll not be rid of me so easily. I plan to see this through."

"Your funeral," Ophelia said. "That goes for the rest of you, I suppose."

"I think we are all committed," Abigail said.

Sofia nodded in agreement. "Yes. It feels..."

"Right," Elizabeth finished.

The group finished their meal, packed up and returned to the trail. They rode quietly through the warm morning. Elizabeth stayed directly behind whoever rode point, typically Ophelia or Abigail. Riding one of the spare horses, Kira galloped ahead from time to time, scouting for the various dangers of New Mexico Territory. Sofia continued to read, trusting her horse to follow the others. Elizabeth hoped they didn't suffer a sudden emergency because the extra seconds it would take for Sofia to react could be the difference between life and death. Clara chatted with anyone who would ride close to her, mostly Maria.

They stopped in a little oasis, refilled their canteens and watered the horses and mule before riffling through saddle bags for quick trail food.

Elizabeth decided the time had come to ask Kira some questions. She approached the young woman. "You promised to explain about the beast lurking around Tierra de Cobre."

Kira's eyes widened. She checked the position of the sun before speaking. "There is an old god of the lands south of here. She is called by many names. Matlazihua. X'tabay. And she is said to lure men to their doom with her voice. They say when she reveals her face, it is like a horse's skull, though sometimes she appears as an ancient woman, withered and wrinkled. I have seen her from a distance, but only from behind. I cannot tell you what face she wears in Tierra de Cobre."

Sofia joined them, followed by the others. "There are similar tales in Spain."

"Perhaps she came with the Spaniards. Or this Spanish creature merged with something even older. The strongest of the wise and powerful from a dozen different peoples chased her from the lands south of here a century ago and trapped her underground."

"And what happens to the men she takes?" Maria asked.

"It is said she devours their spirit—souls, as the blue robes call it," Kira said. "She devours it and enslaves their bodies for whatever purpose she desires."

Maria nodded. "And women?"

"She wields no power to control women, though if a woman goes to her willingly and offers herself, she will be changed and become a dark daughter of the monster with some of the same powers and hunger, though lesser."

"I've read of this creature," Sofia said softly. "The description matches the Sihuanaba, one of several old gods of the land." Sofia glanced at the other women. "While it might not be able to control women, we are not invulnerable to its other powers or a physical attack."

Elizabeth was interested in the beast's history but

wanted to know its weaknesses. "And do the stories tell how to stop her? What magics they used to bind her?"

"No," Kira said, shaking her head. "But my people say the monster is weakened in the presence of copper. If the miners and men of this village released her, she must be stopped before she creates daughters and sends them across the land. Once strong enough, she will take her thralls and spread her control to the pillars of the world."

"These other powers you mentioned. What are we facing?" Ophelia asked.

"First, we should determine if this is the beast," Sofia replied. "No point in preparing for something we might not face."

On that grim note, the group packed up and climbed into their saddles. Ophelia and Elizabeth shared a long look before the women rode on toward Tierra de Cobre.

MARIA RODE in the back of the group, letting Clara chat with Elizabeth. Ophelia rode past her, heading to take over point, while Abigail began to drop back. The gunfighter paused next to Maria.

"I must say, Maria, despite the young Apache's tale, I am still dubious."

Maria cocked her head, narrowed her eyes. "And yet the men are gone."

"Could be a natural explanation. I will need to see this for myself."

"There are more things under heaven and earth, Abbie," Sofia, riding just ahead of them, said without looking up from her book.

Maria smiled at Abigail. "Abbie?"

Abigail blushed. "I'd rather not be called that anymore if you please."

"As you wish," Sofia said as she turned a page.

"Abbie?" Maria asked again.

"I was—younger and much more innocent in those days."

Maria nodded. "I think it's a good name."

"Do you?"

"Yes."

Abigail smiled at Maria. "Well. That's something to consider."

Maria watched the gunfighter drop to the rear of their little party, falling back enough to make sure something wasn't sneaking up on them. She gave the woman a considering look over her shoulder before turning to face forward.

There was something about Abigail she found exciting. Maybe it was the other woman's polite nature, the danger lurking under the surface, or just that Abigail was attractive and dressed like a somewhat dapper man, but Maria felt lighter, more comfortable with Abigail than the others.

She had never seriously considered taking a woman as her lover before, though she'd thought about it a few times. But her family expected her to marry and she wanted children. Esteban had been a good man, if traditional and unimaginative. Decent, hardworking, and as exciting as wet laundry. They'd been hoping to have children, both wanting a family. She thanked a God she wasn't sure she believed in anymore that they had failed and shuddered at the thought of dealing with this monster pregnant or with a young child on her hip.

I'm being ridiculous about Abigail Long, Maria thought. She'd known Abigail for two entire days. Maybe she was just lonely. Maybe she wanted the comfort of a touch. Her late husband had been a gentle man and she missed that about him. More than Esteban himself, she realized.

She knew exactly what the priest would say about her desires concerning Abigail Long, but God hadn't saved the priest from the monster destroying her village, so she wasn't particularly inclined to worry much about his opinion now.

But she wondered what Abigail would say.

Best to keep such thoughts to herself, Maria decided. In a few days, they would either be dead, or if they destroyed the beast, these women would be moving on to the next town, new adventures, jobs.

They stopped to rest before making a final push to Tierra de Cobre. Maria studied the others. Clara bent over her notebook, writing at a furious pace with her pencil. Sofia continued to read. Elizabeth prayed, rosary in her hands. Kira moved away from the group, carrying her rifle, watching outward. Ophelia rested with her back to a rock, hat over her eyes. Abigail cleaned her pistol with a cloth.

Maria gave her horse more attention than necessary before they rode out. They'd be in Tierra de Cobre in a few more hours, planning to face down a monster. Maria took a series of slow breaths. Now was not the time for flights of fancy. Returning to her home filled her with a dread she would never admit to these strangers. Part of her wished she'd stayed behind in Magdalena as well, but she could not—would not—send strangers to fight for her town and not defend it herself.

She approached the group. "We should skirt around the mine. I know it will need exploring at some point, but I'd rather we make a plan in town first." Maria licked her lips. "I don't want to be near the mine or the creek after nightfall."

Ophelia tipped her hat up. "Sensible."

"Agreed," Elizabeth added.

Maria withheld an internal sigh. "Okay. I can guide us to the fastest trail around them."

Kira swung up onto her horse. "I will ride up front with you."

AN EERIE HUSH held the streets of Tierra de Cobre tight in its grip as the seven women rode into the town. A scattering of lights shone in the restaurant and hotel, but everything else stood silent. The silence felt ominous, but Maria heard Daisy's owl call as they approached, so she knew the women were being cautious about the unknown riders. "Hello! Temperance! Anyone! I've brought help."

Slowly, the townswomen emerged from the buildings and nearby streets. A few carried lanterns. All of them bore weapons. They converged on the seven.

Temperance, shotgun nestled in her arms, stepped to the front. "Maria, welcome back. Where are Charlotte and Anna-Beth?"

"They stayed behind." A murmur rose among the townswomen. Maria could taste the panic. Losing two of their leaders stressed the fragile alliance of the remaining residents to near breaking.

Elizabeth nudged her horse forward next to Maria. The women quieted. "I am Elizabeth. This," she said, turning in the saddle, "is my partner Ophelia. These others are Abigail Long, Sofia Podany, Kira of the Badlands, and Clara Dashelle. Maria brought us here to help you defeat the beast attacking your village."

Rachel Owens moved up next to Temperance. "There's only six of you."

"Seven," Maria corrected. "And all of you."

"Us?" Rachel shook her head. "We aren't soldiers or gunfighters."

"No," Elizabeth said. "You are something better and stronger. You are women fighting for your homes. If you trust us, we will help you fight. Teach you to fight if necessary."

"But first, our guests need to rest," Maria said. "It's been a long, hard ride, and they need food and warm beds."

"I'm Temperance," Maria's friend said in welcome, breaking the tension. "Thank you for helping Tierra de Cobre. Let's get you fed and settled."

Ophelia swung down from her saddle. "Please. Tomorrow, we can plan, look at your mine, scout the creek, and decide what's needed."

Maria led the group to the single hotel in town, a two-story building, square with a false front and two chairs on the porch. Inside, the tiny parlor boasted wooden chairs and a few small tables near the front windows. The women unloaded their gear, and Maria turned the animals over to Daisy, promising she'd be along to help her with them in a few minutes. An elderly man, stooped with age and bald, greeted them.

It took a few minutes to sort out rooms. Maria had worried that George might hesitate to give rooms to Ophelia and Kira. The innkeeper stared hard at the two women before shrugging and passing everyone the keys.

Kira cleared her throat. "I do not need a room."

Clara turned to Kira. "Oh? Where do you plan to sleep?"

"Not trapped in a building."

"Be safe," Sofia said. She reached out and briefly placed a hand on the younger woman's shoulder, withdrew it.

"No one is safe." Kira nodded to the other women and left the hotel with her meager possessions in her arms, rifle slung over her shoulder.

Maria worried poor old George would die of heart failure or exhaustion if he tried going up and down the stairs carrying everyone's gear. She needed a way to save the old man's pride without offending him. Fortunately, the other women could also see the problem.

"Thank you, sir. I'll see to my bags," Abigail said.

"Yes, I'm fine as well," Clara added. Maria saw the woman's grip tightening on the small crate's handle.

"Perhaps you could show us to our rooms, though?" Elizabeth said. She and Ophelia were carrying their possessions too.

George smiled and waved at them to follow him up the stairs. Sofia allowed the man to carry her smaller bag up— just enough effort to make the old man feel useful.

Maria stayed behind as they all vanished up the stairs. She still needed to help Daisy with the horses and mule, but she needed the latest gossip, and Temperance was standing right there. "Any news?"

"A couple more of them walking corpses wandered into town last night. None of ours. We took care of them, but it spooked everyone."

"Damn."

"They came armed, Maria. They came in shooting but moved slowly, twitching like puppets on a string. They didn't hit anyone, so we got lucky."

She sighed. "I fear there will be blood spilled and more death before the end. Any other bad news?"

"The Clancy boy broke out of his momma's cellar, said he could hear her--and by her, I'm guessing the thing at the creek--call and needed to answer. We managed to stop him. He's locked in the jail with Romo." Temperance licked her lips. "The others we'd saved managed to escape."

"Honestly, it is a miracle we've saved a few men. It is a miracle none of us left behind have been killed," Maria said.

"Maria? These women, you figure they can help?"

Maria frowned. "Yes, I do."

"And if they can't?"

"If not, I think we are all doomed."

CHAPTER

NINE

"Oh. Hello."

Kira looked down the barrel of her rifle at the young woman climbing into the church bell tower, her rifle slung over her shoulder. Kira had set up an elevated cold camp, offering a good field of view covering the entire town and the various dirt tracks. She mainly wanted to watch the roads leading to the mine and the creek.

The top of the little mission church seemed perfect. She should have guessed others had the same idea. She heard the owl call as they rode into town, and while it was good mimicry, Kira knew it was no owl. She should have expected another would climb up to this spot.

And now she was pointing her rifle at one of the locals. She realized this might end badly. "Hello," she responded, then recognized this woman as the one Maria handed the horses and mules over to. She slowly pointed her rifle upward. "I thought I would be alone."

"Well, this is where I stand watch most nights. I can see

nearly the whole town and for miles around. Can I join you?"

"Yes." Kira had expected fear or even anger from the townswoman over having a weapon aimed at her. She was ready to deal with fear and anger. The matter-of-fact attitude startled Kira.

The young woman finished climbing into the tower. In the darkness, Kira could just see that her braided hair was golden. She dressed sensibly in a dark blue blouse tucked into a long dark brown skirt and carried the same Springfield rifle Kira possessed. "Thank you." She took a position where she could watch their surroundings from the shadows. "So, you're here to fight our monster? I mean, I'm just guessing since you rode in with Maria. That Elizabeth woman called you Kira of the Badlands, right?"

"Kira. I am Kira. Yes, I plan to trap or destroy the horror dwelling at your creek or die fighting it to my last breath." The other woman looked at her for several moments. "What?" Kira finally snapped.

"It's just…you don't seem any older than me. But here you are riding into town to fight a monster, with Abigail Long no less."

"You know the gunfighter?"

"I—um—no. I've never met her."

"Then how—"

"Dime novels," the woman blurted out. "Abigail Long is the heroine of three Beadle's dime novels."

Kira laughed. "I wonder if Abigail knows about these."

"Please don't tell her I read them. Please."

"I will keep your secret."

"Thank you. And I'm sorry. I shouldn't have judged you by your age. I mean, here I am in this bell tower with a rifle in my hand, watching the roads for shambling corpses.

I don't know you. I don't know who you are or what you've lived through."

Kira stared at the other woman for several seconds before speaking. "I am Kira of the *Haisndayin*. I was born in these lands before my tribe was killed or fled. I have stolen horses from your blue-coated cavalry and silver from the priests at the missionary school. I have been beaten nearly to death for speaking my own tongue. I have been a slave in a brothel. I have killed men and women to escape and taken their possessions. My grandmother was the last with the knowledge to fight what lurks in the darkness. The knowledge she passed to me is incomplete, but I carry the copper knife and I know that the monster fears copper. I have seen the beast at the flowing water. I must stop her before she spreads darkness into the world. There, now you know me."

"I've seen her too," the other woman said softly. "I've scouted the creek from a distance a few times, close enough to see the monster, far enough away that it didn't notice me."

"Did you see her face?" Kira asked.

"No. Her face stayed hidden by her hair." She shifted positions and moved deeper into the shadows. Kira admired the woman's ability to practically vanish from sight even though she was barely five feet away. "My name is Daisy. It's a flower."

"I know," Kira said. "Your priests educated me."

"Not my priests. I'm Baptist, which I think was Preacher Wilkes's brand, but I'm not much for Sunday church. My folks are buried back in Missouri somewhere and I came here so my aunt and uncle could raise me. Uncle Jackson was the town mayor before the thing took him. I guess my aunt got scared and left town. I was planning to strike out on my own anyway, before all this happened. I'm not the marrying kind, even though my aunt and uncle favored me marrying Preacher Wilkes." Daisy snorted in disdain. "As if I'd marry any of the men around here."

"You could go too," Kira said. "The road to Magdalena is still open for now."

"I could," Daisy agreed. "Likely should."

"Why don't you?"

"Some of these folks are my friends. I won't abandon them," Daisy said. "I guess my aunt and uncle's place is mine now."

"I refuse to be tied to a place."

"Most folks want to settle somewhere."

Kira snorted. "Settlers. As if the land can ever be owned. Someday, your people's greed will destroy you. I hope you do not finally destroy my people as well."

"I am more worried about the thing at the pond. You think your copper knife can kill it?"

"I know it."

"Even though no one told you it could?"

"I – I believe. I must believe it can kill the thing. Why else would it come to me?"

"Well, Kira, if you think it can kill that thing, I will do my dead-level best to give you that chance. Tell me, where are you staying? Besides in the belfry."

"This belfry."

"Wrong. You're staying with me. Rachel Owens is supposed to be on watch tonight. She'll be along in a few minutes. I'm just covering for her while she puts her kids to bed. I suspect she will not be pleased to share space with you despite you being here to fight for us. When's the last time someone cooked you a decent meal and drew you a hot bath?"

"I've found food enough." Kira paused. "But it has

been some time since I bathed in something other than a creek or lake."

"Well, I know I will want to build a little fire and have a warm bath after dealing with the horses and mule. I reckon we can draw and heat enough water for two. I got a copper tub in a shed behind the house. The only one outside of the hotel. We might as well use it."

Kira would never admit it, but the one thing she missed from her time in El Paso was the baths. She and the other working girls were encouraged to keep themselves clean and tidy. It set them apart from other saloons and houses in town. "I would accept a bath." She felt a smile spread across her lips. "As your guest, I should go first."

Daisy stepped out of the shadows. "Rachel's coming, so we should move. I'll meet her on the ground while you slip away. I'll come find you at the back of the mission." The blonde girl gave Kira a mischievous little smile. "And honestly, why should either of us go last?"

CHAPTER

TEN

Ophelia glanced at the hotel's front door as Maria slipped inside, the young woman scanning the room before joining them. The hotel keeper set up a makeshift dining room in the lobby, where Ophelia, Elizabeth, Abigail, Clara, and Sofia sat. Maria settled at the table as Temperance bustled around, feeding them biscuits, gravy, pork belly, and eggs.

Maria waved off the offered food. "Where is Kira?" she asked, pouring herself a cup of coffee.

"Still sleeping, perhaps?" Clara said.

Ophelia frowned. "That girl didn't strike me as the late-morning type."

"And I doubt she's fled," Elizabeth said. "She may just be waiting to join us once we've started moving about town."

As if speaking her name summoned her, Kira opened the hotel door, held it for Daisy to enter, and followed. Ophelia noted Kira looked cleaned up and mildly pleased about something. She wore fresh clothing, and her braid was in a style Ophelia suspected Daisy had given her.

Daisy gave everyone a challenging glare as she followed Kira into the room.

Temperance waved them over to the table. "Good morning. I was wondering where you'd wandered off to, Daisy-girl."

Daisy, who'd stopped to stare at Abigail Long, blinked and blushed. "Sorry, ma'am. I got distracted."

"My fault," Kira said. "That coffee smells good."

Ophelia pushed a cup toward an empty chair. Kira settled and poured a cup as Daisy moved to help Temperance by keeping everyone's cups full of hot coffee and tea.

Elizabeth cleared her throat. "I plan to explore your mine."

Maria nodded agreement over the cup of coffee Abigail passed to her. "I will lead you there."

"You pointed at it when we rode around it last night. I think I can find it again." Ophelia pointed in the general direction of the mine with her fork.

"And?"

Ophelia shrugged. "I am just saying, Maria Garcia, there isn't any need for you to put yourself in danger."

"It is my choice," Maria said.

Ophelia lifted her coffee cup in a small salute. "Fair enough."

The room grew quiet except for the soft tinkling of forks on plates and the swish of more coffee being poured.

Sofia wiped her mouth with her napkin and set the linen on her empty plate. "Should we all come to the mine, or is this more of a scouting mission?"

The table grew quiet as the women looked for someone to decide. Ophelia glanced at Elizabeth. "I think we can divide our labor today," Elizabeth said. "Ophelia and I will look at your mine. Maria will be our local guide. Kira should join us since she carries some knowledge of the beast."

"If you wish," Kira whispered. Daisy touched Kira's shoulder before starting to clear the dishes.

Abigail poured the last of the coffee into her cup. "Seems reasonable. I'll start working with the other women to set up a defense of the town."

"I can assist," Sofia said.

Temperance set a fresh pot of coffee on the table and leaned into the conversation. "I'll introduce you around."

"And what shall I do?" Clara asked. "I'd love to come along to the mine."

Ophelia opened her mouth to retort and stopped at a glance from Elizabeth.

"I would appreciate it if you would talk with folks here in town," Elizabeth said. "Find out everything you can about what happened here. While I believe everything Maria related to us, others might possess different knowledge."

"Ah! You want me to interview the people. Of course."

Everyone finished breakfast. *Time to get moving,* Ophelia thought. "Shall we, ladies?"

The women finished their drinks and rose, checking weapons and other necessary items.

Ophelia watched as Daisy stepped up to Kira, taking one of her hands.

"Don't die," Daisy said.

"I always try not to die."

Ophelia saw the look of confusion on Clara's face at Kira and Daisy's interaction as if trying to decide what was happening. Before Ophelia could say anything, Kira turned to Clara. "It is important to recognize when life offers you a bit of happiness and to be sensible enough to accept it."

Clara blinked in confusion before understanding blossomed, and she blushed. Ophelia chuckled as she started to follow Elizabeth and Maria out the door. She noticed Clara glance between Kira and Daisy and blush again.

Sofia stepped between Kira and Clara with a smirk. "Stop torturing her, *o prietenă*. We've matters to attend to."

Ophelia shook her head. Clara was surely getting her horizons broadened. She hoped the young reporter survived to take her new perspectives into the world.

Ophelia and her three companions spent little enough time saddling their horses and riding out to the mine, following the wagon track heading in the same direction. She was glad they weren't traveling like the miners must have every morning. She'd bet her last silver nickel the transport wagon was a bumpy, rough ride. Their horses would carry them to safety faster if things went south, and in their line of work, things tended to go wrong at the slightest turn.

They rode to the mouth of the mine and tied the horses to a rickety hitching rail. As one, they stood silently in front of the abandoned mine for a few moments. The transport wagon lay on its side just off the track. An ore car designed to be pulled by mule sat near the mouth of the mine on narrow rails. A couple of hundred yards or so from the mine sat buildings, and equipment Ophelia figured might be the smelter.

"Well," Ophelia said, "at least we aren't being attacked."

"A pleasant change," Elizabeth replied. "Maria, would you say the trouble is more active at night?"

"Yes. They attacked the town twice."

"Attacked?" Ophelia asked.

Maria turned to her. "Temperance said a couple of the

possessed men came to town twice, seeking the rest of the men and boys. The women destroyed them."

"At least the women of Tierra de Cobre will fight." Ophelia turned her attention back to the mouth of the mine. "I suppose we need to check it out."

"I do not wish to go under the ground." Kira bit her bottom lip. "It is no place for the living."

Elizabeth reached out and touched Kira's arm. "I will not ask anyone to follow me, but I must go below. This is where it began, and I must see."

Ophelia spat on the ground and adjusted her weapons, drew the shotgun from her back, opened it, checked the loads, and snapped it shut. "Let's get this foolishness over with."

Elizabeth smiled at her. "We will also seek out the beast's lair by the water in a day or two."

"One damned thing at a time, Beth." Ophelia walked into the mine, the others trailing behind her.

ABIGAIL STOOD in front of the gathered townswomen, Temperance at her side. The women of Tierra de Cobre carried a hodgepodge of rifles and shotguns and looked nervous, but determined. Abigail glanced at Clara. She wasn't sure of the young reporter's part in all this, but she'd come this far, so Abigail gave the woman the benefit of the doubt. She turned her attention back to the gathered women.

"I won't insult you by asking if you can use those weapons," Abigail said. "Either you can, or you can't, and there isn't time to teach you. Stay if you know how to use your weapons and think you can fight. Otherwise, I can find different jobs for you such as tending the wounded, reloading weapons, other duties."

The townswomen murmured, but none of them moved to leave.

Good enough, Abigail thought. "I know y'all been keeping watch, but I want to set up a formal schedule so there's always someone alert for trouble. You'll work in teams of four, two sets of partners. Watchers will need to be awake and alert during their watch. We will set one pair to watch the approaches to town, the other to patrol the streets."

"Seems reasonable," Temperance agreed.

Abigail gave the street a critical look. "Now, as to how we will set up our defenses. If what I'm hearing is true, the real trouble will come from the creek, so we'll set up some barricades using wagons and barrels and whatnot on the trail leading into town. We'll set up lighter positions on the road from the mine." Abigail peered down the street. "Once we have better information, we should also set a few traps. Now, tell me what places we could hide anyone unable or unwilling to fight."

Sofia walked down the dusty street, trailing behind Kira's friend. *Daisy, that is the girl's name.* Daisy led her toward a square adobe building next to the marshal's office. The building's door was made of iron bars and it sported one small window, also set with iron bars. This was the local jail where the women of Tierra de Cobre held two men who labored under the beast's call. Sofia gripped her small handbag and stopped a few feet from jail door. The building must be miserable and hot during the summer, she thought.

Inside the jail sat a young man, little more than a boy, brown-haired, bucked-toothed, and pale-faced. She guessed him to be about fifteen. The dark-skinned older man in his late forties or early fifties in the cell with him looked up at her approach.

"Gentlemen," Sofia said.

The older man stepped up to the jail door. "*Señora.* Are you come to free us?"

"If by free, you mean cut off from the song of the fiend, yes."

"You need to let us out," the boy said. "We need to—come on Daisy, you know me. I'm your friend. Let us out, Daisy."

The teenager frowned at them. "I'm not letting either of you out, so just put that thought away right now, William Clancy."

"None of you will be leaving this building until I break the *geas* upon you," Sofia said.

"We hear her," the older man said. "We must go to her. She calls us. Please."

Sofia studied the prisoners for several moments before opening her bag and searching until she found the two brown bottles she wanted. She handed one of them to Daisy. "When I hold out my hand, open the bottle and pour a few drops into my palm. Do you understand?"

Daisy took the bottle. "Yes, ma'am."

Such a solemn youngster, Sofia thought. "Be brave, my child." Sofia opened the second bottle and poured a white powder into her hand. She stepped toward the jail, stopping just out of reach of the men inside.

She lifted her palm and stared at the men. "*Dezvălui.*" She blew the powder at the two men. They backed away, snarling and hissing. William, his face twisted in a monstrous expression, lunged at Sofia, reaching through the bars for her.

Sofia held out her hand to Daisy. "Quickly."

Daisy opened the bottle with the barest fumbling and poured a bit of liquid into Sofia's hand. Striking snake-fast, Sofia grabbed William's wrist and pulled him forward while stepping closer to him. She reached through the bars and touched his face with the hand holding the liquid.

William screamed, high and wild, eyes turning black and going wide as Sofia held him in place with an iron grip. A trail of smokey lines poured out of William's eyes and mouth, moving past Sofia and Daisy.

Releasing William's wrist and stepping away from the jail, Sofia turned and studied the lines traveling out of town. She snatched at the wisps of smoke and twisted, snapping them. William collapsed to the ground, panting, and began to cry. A high-keening noise filled the air as the smoke dissipated.

Sofia smiled and turned to Daisy, who stared at her with wide eyes. "Rejoice, child. I do not know about the men the monster has already taken, but we can save these two once the beast is destroyed."

THE WOMEN GATHERED in the town square preparing to defend Tierra de Cobre heard the keening and some of them dropped their weapons and fled.

Abigail looked toward the direction of the unholy howl. "Sweet Jesus."

"What is it?" Clara stepped to Abigail's side.

"Damned if I know, Miss Dashelle, but we'd best be ready for trouble." She turned to the remaining women. "Everyone, pick a spot with some cover."

Abigail walked down the street, Clara trailing in her wake.

"Do you have a plan?" Clara asked.

"Miss Dashelle, are you armed? Something a little more deadly than a pencil on your person?"

"Of course. I'm not an idiot." Settling her open bag in the nook of her elbow, she drew a Remington double barrel derringer from inside, switched it to her other hand, and retrieved a Barlow knife from the bag, both weapons pearl-handled and ornate. She set the bag on the ground. "Will these suffice?"

"They'll be good enough."

Abigail turned toward the pond. She wished her companions would come riding up from the copper mine, ready to help her with whatever might be coming. She wished Sofia stood next to her. Even if she didn't believe in this supposed monster, she knew the reality of magic. You couldn't be around Sofia Podany without seeing magic in person: genuine, real magic.

As if thinking about her was a summoning, Sofia appeared from a side street, Daisy at her side.

"I'm guessing you know what caused the hell-shriek?" Abigail said.

"Yes. The power our unknown fiend wields over mortal men is not absolute. It can be broken. The beast was unhappy when I broke off the enchantment on one of the men in the prison."

Abigail snorted in laughter. "You never do things by halves, do you? Should we rally the rest of our companions before the thing sweeps down on us in retribution?"

Sofia frowned. Abigail thought she might be looking at something in the distance only she could see. "No. I suspect it will try to scout us first by cover of night."

"It's always at night," Abigail muttered.

"Why?" Clara asked.

Sofia shrugged. "Some monsters cannot abide the light. Or it is because they know we fear the dark, are more vulnerable at night." She smiled at Abigail. "How goes turning our flock of desert doves into a fighting force?"

Abigail glanced over her shoulder at the woman who had chosen to fight. Temperance, shotgun at the ready, stood a dozen or so paces between Abigail and the women of Tierra de Cobre. A handful stood steady behind Temperance; a few others peeked up from their cover, weapons clutched in their hands. She would work with these women. The rest could reload guns, tend to the wounded, or hide away in the cellars. "If nothing else, the shriek quickly weeded out the ones who won't stand and fight."

"Yes, several of them did run screaming at the first sign of trouble," Clara said.

"Glad I could help find the fighters among them." Sofia turned to Daisy. "Come, we must prepare." Without another word, Sofia walked toward the saloon, Daisy trailing in her wake.

Abigail allowed herself a moment of amusement before turning back to her designated task. She needed to take the remaining women in hand. As for the others…

"Miss Dashelle—"

"Please, just call me Clara."

"Clara, could you please find and collect the women who aren't ready to face danger directly? We can still form them into something useful, I hope."

"I—yes. Yes, I can do that."

"Clara."

"Yes?"

Abigail smiled at Clara. "You did well. You held your

nerve in the face of danger. You stayed steady. I won't over-look you or underestimate you."

Clara blushed. "Thank you."

THE THING ELIZABETH hadn't counted on upon entering a recently active mine for the first time was how the rough rock walls and various timbers at all odd angles distorted her senses, making the world feel chaotic and causing a rush of vertigo. She paused for a few minutes to allow the feeling to pass before walking deeper into the mine.

"We'll need light soon," Ophelia said. "I wish we'd brought torches."

"I live here and didn't think of it either," Maria said.

"You haven't spent much time in this mine, I'm guess-ing," Ophelia replied.

"Truthfully, none."

Elizabeth lifted her rosary, crucifix dangling. "Not to worry." The crucifix began to glow brightly, cast a beam of light ahead of them, beating back the darkness.

"You are a light unto the world," Maria whispered, awestruck.

"Well, at least unto this mine," Elizabeth chuckled.

The four women moved deeper into the cool dark, following the main shaft. The air grew oppressive, the walls rougher. They climbed over fallen timber and began to find abandoned equipment: picks, hammers, an ore car left half-loaded with raw copper. They reached a branching off deep under the ground, a side shaft leading down. Eliza-beth paused a moment, deciding between the main shaft or the new branch, and chose to follow the new branch.

If the main shaft felt oppressive, the branch pressed her senses with ominous energy. She couldn't fathom why the miners dug in this direction. Surely, they'd sensed it too, a dark, oily dread rising in her mind. She glanced over her shoulder at her companions, each cast in the eerie glow of the light coming from her crucifix. Ophelia clutched her shotgun, looking grim. She caught Elizabeth's eyes and shook her head. Maria chewed her bottom lip, one hand on the rough walls. Kira's eyes widened, and Elizabeth thought the young woman might panic and flee at any moment. She would not blame Kira if she did. Elizabeth's senses screamed, 'Run, you fool, run!' But she pushed forward.

Picking her way around the clutter and debris, Elizabeth pushed another twenty yards into the shaft before she stopped, the stench of broken magic pushing against her magical senses. She muttered a prayer to her guardian angels as she raised the rosary. The silver light intensified, illuminating the scene of wreckage before her. Behind her, Ophelia swore softly, and Kira cried out in her people's tongue. She felt movement at her side.

"What happened here?" Maria whispered.

Elizabeth took a series of deep breaths. She'd long grown accustomed to the smell of death, and these corpses, what remained, were well past the most putrid stage. They'd blasted away a section of wall and, in the blasting, opened a chamber lined with a rich vein of copper, a mixture of the classic copper color one expected and a deep verdigris. Elizabeth stepped deeper into the chamber, Maria at her side. She could see the image of a human shape indented in the rock. Elizabeth thought Sofia might spot something she'd missed, but the basics were easy enough for her to interpret.

"This is where Kira's ancestors trapped it," Elizabeth said, eyes scanning the wall for more clues. "The copper must act as a barrier, sealed with their power to trap the beast."

"And the miners blasted open the trap," Ophelia said.

"Yes," Elizabeth agreed. "I suspect a small crack in the wall, a place where the magic and copper weakened, allowed it to reach out to their minds. Once that happened, they were all doomed." She glanced at Maria. "Do you recognize any of them?"

"Yes," Maria whispered. "I will—I will tell their widows."

"Why did it kill these men instead of taking them?" Ophelia asked.

"It needed their life energy after being so long trapped, I suspect." Elizabeth frowned at Maria.

"I have resigned myself to Esteban's death," Maria answered the unasked question.

The high wailing, though muffled underground, reached them. The hairs along Elizabeth's arms rose as her heart beat faster.

"We must return to the surface!" Kira called. "We cannot be trapped here."

"Go!" Ophelia called out, giving Elizabeth a tug on the arm to get her moving.

Elizabeth let Ophelia, shotgun at the ready, lead them out of the mine. She occasionally glanced behind her, making sure they weren't being followed, making sure Maria, guarding the rear, fled with them.

They broke out into the light. Elizabeth sighed with relief, pleased at the lack of immediate danger. Wary and weary, the four women mounted their nervous horses and made haste for Tierra de Cobre.

Ophelia took the lead, with Elizabeth dropping back behind her. This was their agreed-upon way. If running toward danger, Ophelia rode ahead of Elizabeth. If running away, Ophelia covered the rear. Elizabeth spared a glance over her shoulder. Kira was gaining on Elizabeth, with Maria watching behind them, pistol in one hand.

As they closed on the town, they could see Abigail, Sofia, and several other women waiting for them. With no sign of danger, Ophelia slowed their headlong charge until all four rode abreast.

Elizabeth looked at her partner. "It seems we are not being attacked despite the terrifying screech."

Ophelia gave her a crooked smile. "I'll take any victory we can get."

Elizabeth turned back toward the waiting town. She wondered how many more victories were in their future.

CHAPTER

ELEVEN

"A part of me," Elizabeth said, "wants to be angry and chastise you, but we are both adults, and your methods taught us something important." She set her empty teacup on the round table and looked deeply into Sofia's eyes, once again trying to take the measure of the woman.

Sofia smiled over her cup of tea. "I admit I am sometimes impulsive."

"Are we expecting an attack?" Maria asked. She glanced out the hotel window and frowned. "Should we prepare?"

Ophelia, sitting next to Elizabeth, shrugged. "Yes, we should. Though I agree with Abigail and Sofia. I suspect it will be more of a scouting thrust."

"Yes," Elizabeth agreed. "I feel this first encounter will test our strength and resolve." She turned back to Sofia. "Your thoughts on our findings in the mine?"

The sorceress frowned. "Kira said copper would be key to trapping or destroying the beast. I will need to see it to

83

understand completely, but yes, I think you are correct in your assessment of what happened in the mine."

"A shame we have no copper bullets," Maria said. "Those might stop the beast."

Ophelia chuckled and lifted her cup of coffee to her lips, pausing. "I have a few, along with several silver bullets and a handful of gold ones." She took a long sip of her coffee and regarded the other women. "Some creatures can't be dealt with by lead."

"But we can still destroy the undead men with lead, yes?" Sofia asked.

"Yes," Maria replied. "Though we've needed headshots to kill them."

"If we can find any men who are being controlled but still are alive, we should attempt to capture them," Sofia said. "I might be able to save them."

Elizabeth licked her lips. "You said you might be able to save them. Is it possible you might fail?"

"It all depends on how much of their self remains."

Maria glanced out the window again and frowned. "The ones we've encountered seemed to be mindless puppets. There was no saving them."

"We could load scatterguns with raw copper bits. There's enough of it just lying around outside the mine." Ophelia smiled. "Hell, we could load up pennies."

"A sensible plan which keeps us out of the mine itself," Elizabeth agreed. "Mrs. Garcia, you keep looking out the window and frowning. Is there a problem?"

"If you consider your reporter friend having climbed the mission belfry a problem."

Elizabeth beat Ophelia and Sofia to the window. In the bell tower, Clara Dashelle tied string or wire to the four corners of the belfry. Daisy was working with Clara, occasionally handing Clara tools.

"What the devil is she up to?" Ophelia muttered.

"Only one way to find out," Elizabeth replied. "Ladies, follow me." She moved swiftly out the door into the street, not bothering to check if the others followed. By the time Elizabeth ended her purposeful march to the mission, a dozen other women walked at her heels. She stopped at the base of the adobe mission and looked up at Clara and Daisy. "Miss Dashelle," she called out, "what on Earth are you doing?"

Clara smiled brightly down at her. "Oh! Hello, Miss Elizabeth. I needed some place high to set up my wireless. Daisy suggested this belfry. It's quite perfect, and I can string my transmitting wires in a nice little box."

"I'm sorry, Miss Dashelle. A wireless?"

Clara nodded, her smile widening. "Yes. A wireless telegraph. How did you think I managed to send my dispatches so quickly to the newspaper?"

"May I come up and look at it?"

Clara's smile turned slightly brittle, obviously not wanting to give up her secret. "Well, yes. But only you, please." She took a deep breath. "The inventor doesn't want me sharing the technology broadly yet. Please."

Elizabeth turned to the crowd. "Everyone should go about their business, I think." The group of women broke up and drifted away. Satisfied, Elizabeth steeled herself and entered the long, narrow mission.

The tiny vestibule felt forlorn to her: the wooden baptismal bowl empty, the paschal candle a nub. The nave held the required, if crudely created, plaques for the stations of the cross. Elizabeth guessed the nave would hold thirty or so worshipers when it was full.

The sanctuary and tabernacle were surprisingly ornate for such a small congregation, ornamented with actual gold and copper and marble. The altar rested uncovered, though, and the sanctuary lamp hung dark. She supposed without a priest or monk to manage the mission, things fell apart.

She sought the ladder to the belfry, ignoring all the crucifixes, icons, and statues as each representation of Christ, Mary, St. Joseph, and the other saints turned to regard her with sad, solemn eyes. She didn't need their attention or reminder that she had fallen. She knew they would try to call her home. She knew she could never return.

Fortunately, the ladder was conspicuous. Turning her back on the watching eyes, Elizabeth climbed, reached the open hatch, and stepped into the evening sunlight.

"Ah," Clara said as Elizabeth stood, giving the panoramic view of the town, mine, creek, and local geography a good look. "Elizabeth. Yes. Thank you for not pressing the issue and allowing more people to come gawk."

"I see no reason for any but those who need the knowledge of this wireless to bother you. I want to assess if it's a tool we can use to defeat our enemy."

"Oh. Well, I doubt my little bit of gadgetry would help in the coming battle."

"Still," Elizabeth replied.

Clara nodded. "Yes. I suppose." Clara pointed at the mechanism resting on the wooden case she'd protected so carefully.

A bronze device of gears, glass tubes, and various knobs and switches on a brass body rested on the case, a body dominated by a large wheel at the top and a crank handle on one side. A smaller wheel held a spool of narrow paper and there was a standard telegraph key was connected to the device. Thin copper wire ran from a pair of screws to the key, the same copper wire Clara and Daisy had strung around the four corners of the belfry.

"How does it work?" Elizabeth asked.

Clara licked her lips, excited to be able to demonstrate her wireless. "It's remarkably like a normal telegraph. You crank the dynamo to power it up." She began turning the crank handle. A low whine filled the air with each revolution, though Elizabeth could see no other effect. None of the gears turned, nor did the large wheel. Clara wound the machine for two minutes. "When you've powered it up, you release the wheel brake." Clara twisted a knob and pulled it toward her.

The machine instantly sprang to life, the top wheel spinning rapidly. The machine clicked and clacked, and the glass tubes lit up. Elizabeth could feel a shift in the energy in the air, even as Daisy gasped and stared at the machine with wide eyes.

"Now, it works like a normal wired telegraph," Clara said. "I can send a message to any wireless station within range." She picked up a small notebook, not her usual one. "This contains a timetable of when various stations will be powered up and receiving. Once I've made contact, I can request they forward my message until it reaches my home station in Philadelphia. I can also add times when I can receive replies to the end of any message, power up, and receive those messages printed on the paper."

Elizabeth frowned. "I'd think sending an entire news article would take most of a day to tap out."

"It would," Clara agreed. "We've developed a short-hand code to work alongside the Morse. I've memorized the entire code book."

"Ah."

"And I can hook directly to a traditional wired tele-graph as needed." She paused. "There are machines able to send voice messages through the ether, but they're short-ranged and expensive."

"Are there any stations in range, here?"

Clara regarded her little book and flipped a few pages. "Yes. Albuquerque. Amarillo. Colorado City. Santa Fe."

"Santa Fe?"

"Yes."

Elizabeth leaned toward Clara. "Miss Dashelle, might I ask a small favor? One to aid our situation?"

CHAPTER

TWELVE

"Ladies, I understand your need, but I am not a priest. I cannot give the sacrament of penance, nor can I give you absolution." Elizabeth frowned. "I am not even a Sister of Charity anymore."

Maria stared Elizabeth down. "We need this."

Behind Maria stood a dozen or so women, some of whom looked like they could have been Maria's family and a couple of others who resembled Kira, and Grethe Ziegler, who spoke German, a little English, and nothing else. They all wanted to confess their sins before whatever was coming, and she could not give these women what they wanted most.

"We need you to hear our confessions. Even if you can't offer absolution, you can at least personally forgive us," Maria countered.

Elizabeth looked from the assembled women to the various icons, statues, and plaques. She felt their gaze. It weighed on her soul. Steeling herself, she looked up at the watching eyes, asking for guidance, for permission. For forgiveness. She dared not look up at the crucifix, instead

89

focusing her gaze on the statue of the Virgin. A small smile crossed the statue's lips. The Virgin nodded her head, oh so subtly, at Elizabeth.

Hear them, Elizabeth heard in her mind. *Help them. Hold them in your heart. Forgive them their sins as we will forgive them. Sister, come home.*

Elizabeth sighed and turned back to Maria. If she could not offer these women absolution, she would give them what she could. It would be enough for these women to confess their sins before God, Mary, and the saints. As for herself, she had made her choices and had no shame about them. And even if Mary and all the saints would forgive the breaking of her vows to the Church in pursuit of forbidden love, the Church on Earth would never forgive her choices.

"Would you ladies like to confess as a group or individually?" Elizabeth asked.

A soft murmur rose among the women, reminding Elizabeth of schoolgirls caught in some minor transgression. She found it amusing and somewhat charming.

"One at a time, I think," Maria said, deciding for the group.

"Who shall go first?" Elizabeth asked in the exact tone she'd once used on those same errant schoolgirls back in Cincinnati before her fall. .

Maria raised her head. "I will."

Elizabeth and Maria waited for the others to file out of the small mission. Elizabeth stood and beckoned Maria to follow. They both settled on the frontmost pew, a rough, backless wooden bench before the sanctuary.

"I think we can skip all the formalities and rituals and go straight to the point," Elizabeth said. She offered her right hand to Maria, who took it. Elizabeth placed her left hand on top of Maria's. "Now, here before God and

Mother Mary, tell me what troubles your soul, Maria Garcia."

"I am a married woman and feel desire for another."

Elizabeth nodded. "This is understandable. While you have resigned yourself to your husband's death, you do not know if you are a widow or not. If you are a widow, you are free to pursue another, but if not…have you acted upon these desires in the flesh? Or have you but sinned in your heart and mind?"

"Only in my mind, though it is a physical desire."

Elizabeth nodded. "Impure thoughts are not uncommon."

"The person I desire is a woman," Maria blurted out.

"Oh." Elizabeth spared the statue of the Virgin a glance. The smile seemed a little wider, and the expression amused. *I'm so glad you are entertained.* Elizabeth cleared her throat. "Maria, you do understand that the love I bear Ophelia is why I am no longer a Sister of Charity?"

Maria blinked at Elizabeth. "I…Oh. I see."

Elizabeth leaned forward and smiled wider. She gave Maria's hand a little squeeze. "I forgive you your desires."

CHAPTER

THIRTEEN

Ophelia shifted, readjusting her weight from one leg to another. She crouched behind a makeshift barricade of dirt-filled barrels, broken ore carts, and loose timber, watching the road leading from town to the stream-fed pond lair of the monster.

She wished the undead, possessed or whatever they were would just come into town and get it over with. She changed her grip on the shotgun. The group decided to hold off using her actual copper, gold, or silver bullets in what they figured would be a skirmish. They'd save those precious rounds for the main event. Instead, they broke up raw copper and packed it into shotgun loads for Ophelia, Temperance, and a couple of others.

The rest would fight with regular lead, meaning they'd need to demonstrate some serious marksmanship. She figured Abigail and Kira knew how to handle themselves. As for the rest, they would find out soon enough.

They stationed Elizabeth and Sofia on the roof of the hotel so they could wield their magics while being—hope-

92

fully—out of reach. Clara stood on the mission belfry with Daisy, watching the night for trouble. Someone gave Clara a Henry rifle. The young woman looked at it for several minutes before admitting she'd never fired anything bigger than her derringer. Abigail gave Clara a quick lesson on how the rifle worked. Ophelia noted Clara took it seriously, which gave her some hope that the reporter wouldn't accidentally shoot one of them in the confusion of a gun battle. Daisy wielded a Springfield trapdoor, the same rifle as Kira's, and seemed to know how to use it.

Ophelia shifted again, her knees complaining from the enforced immobility. She considered signaling Abigail to call the ambush off, sure the attack wasn't going to materialize, when Daisy hooted from the mission belfry.

The girl sounds like an owl. Ophelia licked her lips and raised her shotgun to the ready.

Eight men, moving stiffly but certainly swifter than she would have expected, entered the town. You could easily mistake them for ordinary men walking down the street under the torchlight Abigail decided to light to help the women see and hit their targets. They could be any group of cowboys coming to town looking for booze and whores, except for the obvious rot and decay.

"Fire!" Abigail called out.

A full two dozen rifles roared to life from various doorways, windows, alleys, and other hidey-holes, peppering the dead men with lead. Ophelia held her fire. She, Temperance, and a few others formed a skirmish line between the street approach to the jail, there to deal with any of the dead who made it past the rifle fire. They'd fight up close with shotguns and pistols, standing between those creatures and the remaining men who'd heard the siren's call.

The dead men—for Ophelia could only think of them

as such—jerked and staggered under the onslaught of lead. She approved of the tactic Abigail chose. She'd opted for a wall of bullets and lucky hits over trying to train them to be sharpshooters. One of the dead men took a round through the head, collapsed, and stayed down.

One down, seven to go.

The remaining seven drew their pistols and returned fire in a slow, methodical way. The women of Tierra de Cobre faltered under the counterattack even as another dead man's head snapped back from a direct hit, and he collapsed.

Some of them are going to break through.

"Behind us!" Clara shouted from the belfry.

Ophelia looked up. Clara raised the Henry rifle to her shoulder and fired. A glance down the street showed they'd been flanked by six more walking dead, heading for the back of the jail. Clara and Daisy both fired again, ducked as one of the dead drew his pistol and replied.

"Hold this line!" Ophelia shouted.

After a nod from Temperance, Ophelia charged toward the dead men, moving to intercept them before they reached the jail. She needed to close on them if she hoped to do any damage with the copper loads. Behind her came the deep roar of another shotgun, followed by the smaller pops of pistols and the cries and screams of wounded women.

One of the dead men faced her and lifted his Colt. Ophelia fired from the hip. The combination of raw copper and pennies ripped into the creature's middle, knocking it to the dirt. She wheeled, fired at another target, and ducked around a building corner before she could see if she'd done any damage, desperate to reach cover and reload.

Pushing two fresh shells into her shotgun, she peered around the corner. Kira flowed ghost-like from the darkness, silent and deadly. The young Apache stabbed one of the dead men in the back of the neck with a dark-bladed knife. The man twitched for a moment before crumbling to dust. The heavy report of Daisy's Springfield echoed from the church belfry, and another undead fell, head blasted off his shoulders. She caught a glimpse of Abigail methodically picking off the slow-moving targets.

An undead man stood at the jail door, trailed by two more dead who had broken past the defenders. Ophelia raised her shotgun, even though she knew the range was too great for her to hit the man. She noticed Temperance and Rachel Owens both giving chase, unwilling to fire, fearful of hitting the men in the jail.

A flash of blue lightning rained down on the two dead men trailing, and they burst into flames. Blinking her eyes to clear them of the dazzling display, she fired once, twice, to no effect, the range too great of any accuracy with her odd loads. She ran toward the man, Kira on her right also moving to stop the potential disaster. A rifle barked, and the dead man's head exploded, body crumbling to the ground.

Ophelia peered around for more danger and found none.

"Clara," Kira called out.

Ophelia looked at the mission belfry. Clara still held the rifle to her shoulder, eyes wide at making the killing shot. A dark stain of blood stood out on her light blue blouse just above her left hip. Clara collapsed.

"Help me!" Daisy cried from the belfry.

Ophelia reached the mission door to find Elizabeth had beaten them all there despite being on a rooftop four buildings away. Sometimes, Ophelia wondered at the speed at which her partner moved. *You'd think her a hawk or raven, flying across the rooftops.* "Clara?" she asked as Elizabeth climbed down the ladder.

"Will survive," Elizabeth assured her.

Figuring Abigail would handle the aftermath of the battle, Ophelia stayed in the mission. She bit her bottom lip as Rachel Owens and Grethe Ziegler carried Clara down the ladder tied to a board. Ophelia moved to the wounded woman's side and took her hand as they carried her toward the hotel. "You did well, Miss Dashelle."

Clara smiled through her pain. "I did, didn't I?"

Ophelia stepped back, allowing Clara to be carried away. She followed them outside into the darkness. Elizabeth moved to her side, reached out, and grasped her hand. "Was this Clara's reason to come?" Ophelia asked. "Is this what you foresaw?"

"No," Elizabeth answered. "But soon she shall fulfill her appointed task."

"Oh?"

"I'm awaiting a reply to a message. Only Miss Dashelle can receive and interpret it."

"Ah." They walked toward the hotel. Ophelia noted with approval that Abigail set sentries to watch, making sure the defenders of Tierra de Cobre were not caught unaware. "Any other killed or wounded besides our Clara?"

"One death, a few others injured, but nothing life-threatening, according to Sofia. I'll check on them in a few hours. First, I need tea and some cake or pastry, whatever our hotel keeper can scare up."

"Used a bunch of energy keeping Clara alive, did you?"

"Yes."

"Elizabeth, something has changed. Those things moved faster than Maria said."

"I'll consult with Sofia and Maria, but I suspect and fear our opponent is gaining power and it is giving her finer control over her thralls."

"Shit."

CHAPTER

FOURTEEN

"I am flattered you asked me, Maria. I just…" Abigail paused.

"No. I understand. I'm sorry."

After battling the walking corpses, after watching men she'd known mindlessly attack their wives and daughters, after watching one of Tierra de Cobre's defenders fall to those same men, the lesson that any one of them might die at any time filled Maria's mind. Nervous and uncertain about what tomorrow might hold, she decided to act. She marched up the steps to Abigail's hotel room, gathered her courage, and knocked on the door.

And now it seemed she'd made a damned fool of herself.

"I'm sorry," Maria repeated. She winced and started to turn away but was stopped by Abigail's gentle touch on her arm.

"Never apologize for being brave. It isn't any reflection on you. You are a courageous and beautiful woman. It is just, I don't desire anyone, man or woman." Abigail gave her a little smile and dropped her hand. "I probably would

98

have made a great nun, except I'm not fond of the idea of a supernatural being ruling my life."

Maria frowned. "That's…unusual."

"I like people. I enjoy being around those I call my friends. I'm just not interested in anything beyond that friendship."

"Are we friends?"

"I believe so, Maria. I would be pleased to call you such if you are amenable to it being the extent of our relationship." Abigail gave her a solemn look. "I know that might be hard after expressing how you feel. But all I can offer you is my friendship."

Maria bit her bottom lip. "Yes. I would like that." Maria settled on the wooden chair in Abigail's hotel room. "Honestly, part of me isn't sure what I'd have done if you had been interested."

Abigail chuckled. "Now I almost wish that I could respond."

"I'd have likely panicked," Maria admitted. She looked around the room and waved at the two books on the dresser. "You must enjoy reading to carry those with you."

"Reading is one of my great pleasures. Do you read?"

"Not much. I struggle to read English, and there are few books in Spanish available. My late husband, Esteban, owned a copy of Lizardi's *El Periquillo Sarniento* and a copy of Dumas' *El Conde de Montecristo*. He would read to me from them sometimes in the evening."

"I'm not familiar with Lizardi," Abigail admitted, "but I enjoy Dumas."

"Do you read Spanish?"

"Sadly, no."

"Pity, I was going to offer his books to you." Maria decided to tease Abigail a little. "Though I have recently learned our Daisy is a reader of dime novels, especially stories set on the frontier, sometimes featuring real living people."

Abigail sighed. "Dear lord. That explains why she keeps giving me big, wide eyes. Perhaps, as my friend, you could explain to her that those tales are at best embellished and at worst outright fictions?"

Maria laughed. "Where would be the fun in that?"

"You seem to spend a lot of time on watch." Kira peered into the night before turning back to Daisy. "I'm beginning to think I made a mistake agreeing to be your watch partner." She looked out at their surroundings again. She was not convinced the fight was over. No one kept count of the undead slain. Kira worried any they missed might be hiding in the darkness, waiting for the town to drop its guard.

"Sorry. The problem is I'm old enough to be responsible but young enough to get bossed around."

"Ill luck that our watch was right after the attack."

Daisy chuckled. "As if either of us would rest after all that action."

"True." She noticed others had gone to their homes and turned out their lights. She would bet her last penny that most of them fell asleep easily enough, exhausted from the night's events.

"Kira."

"Yes?"

"I saw that man turn to dust when you stabbed him in the neck with your copper knife. You were serious when you said you thought the knife could stop the monster. I mean, I believed you, but after seeing what happened, I truly believe it now, if that makes sense?"

Kira bit her bottom lip. She reached into the folds of her garments and drew the knife. "My *shiwóyé*, my grandmother, was the last guardian to hold the knife. I suppose the miners released the beast too quickly for her to act. She was old and sick and hiding in a cave. My *shiwóyé* didn't even tell me how to use the knife before she died. I don't know if there was a special ritual, or if I just stab with it." Kira looked from the knife to Daisy. "I simply have faith in the magic of my ancestors."

"Might be that's all you need," Daisy said. She peered into the surrounding terrain for several seconds. "I think there's one of them out there, watching."

Kira moved next to Daisy. "What did you see?"

"Just a glint of something. Maybe off a buckle. Maybe a movement in the shadows." Daisy frowned. "I could be wrong."

"No, look there," Kira pointed and whispered. "We are being watched. I would not be surprised if she can see through their eyes."

"Should we sound the alarm? If it were just me, I'd call out, but with both of us, maybe we could get help and take care of it without a bunch of fuss?"

"I can sneak up on it, stab it quietly."

"And if there are two of them? Or more? Do you think you could fight five or six at once?"

Kira thought it over for a moment. "You are being sensible. Very well, I'll find one of the others and seek guidance. I'll return."

Daisy lifted her rifle and peered down the barrel. "Hurry. I'll shoot if it moves toward us or back to the pond."

Kira vanished down into the mission and out the door into the dark town. She wanted to find either Sofia or Elizabeth. She found both in the schoolhouse, tending the wounded into the night since they were the closest to a doctor or nurse in town.

Sofia looked up as she entered. "Are we in danger?" She asked.

"We are being watched by at least one of the dead men. He is hiding among the sage and juniper."

"Why didn't you raise the alarm?" Elizabeth asked.

"Daisy and I thought we might be able to sneak up and destroy it." Kira frowned. "I suspect the beast might be able to watch through their eyes."

"Do you know this for a fact?" Sofia asked.

"No," Kira admitted. "But it seems reasonable. Why leave a mindless creature to watch unless you can see what it sees?"

Elizabeth nodded. "A reasonable speculation. One we should act on as if it is fact." She turned to Sofia. "Are you able to assist?"

Sofia nodded. "Yes." She stood and picked up her small bag. "Show me this thrall."

Both women made their way back to the mission. Once in the belfry, they found Daisy still aiming her Springfield into the night. Kira joined her.

"It hasn't moved," Daisy said.

Sofia moved to stand between the two women. "I wonder if this abomination is alone. Shall we find out?"

Before either Kira or Daisy could answer, Sofia knelt and opened her bag. She poked about its contents for a bit, finally producing a clear vial no bigger than her pinkie finger. Sofia stood and looked in the general direction Daisy aimed at. With a grunt, Sofia tossed the vial high into the air ahead of them.

"*Stea Eruptivă!*"

The night sky erupted in a pale silver light. Kira pointed directly at the corpse standing still among the sparse foliage. With the cover of darkness lost, the corpse turned toward the pond, walking away with a shaky but surprisingly quick gait.

"Daisy," Kira said. There was no way they would be able to run the thing down. It would simply take too long to reach a horse. While Kira was an excellent rider, she didn't want to go haring off alone at the enemy camp now that the beast would be alerted.

"Hush," Daisy whispered. She knelt and rested the Springfield atop the tower enclosure to steady her rifle. Kira heard Daisy take a deep breath and slowly let it out. The rifle barked and kicked. Kira watched as the undead man's head disintegrated under the impact of the bullet.

"Well done," Kira said.

Daisy looked over her shoulder. "Thank you."

"There is another," Sofia said, pointing.

This creature was in much worse shape than the first, decomposition slowing its retreat. Kira watched as a hand fell off the thing. She looked down at Daisy.

Daisy reached into her pouch, pulled out a fresh round, ejected the spent one from her rifle, and reloaded as the sounds of shouts and alarms rose in the town around them.

The animated corpse stumbled slowly away as Daisy put three rounds between her fingers at the ready, lifted the rifle, and fired. The bullet blasted through the right shoulder, spinning the corpse-man around. Daisy reloaded and fired again. This round struck the middle of its chest, causing her target to fall backward, shedding skin and organs. Daisy reloaded again as the thing stumbled back to its feet. She fired. The round hit the neck of the thing, severing the head from the body. The shambling corpse collapsed.

Sofia's magical illumination began to flicker before

fading out, leaving the area in darkness again. Sofia looked at the two women. "I suppose you youngsters should make sure of your kill. I'll stay here and watch for more trouble." She smiled softly at them. "Once you are done, you should go and rest."

Kira and Daisy slipped away from the mission as Abigail called up to Sofia, demanding answers. It took the two women nearly twenty minutes to find the creature's remains, tracking it with their noses more than their eyes. Daisy stood with her rifle tucked under her arm, kerchief around her nose and mouth to filter out the worst of the smell. Kira knelt and rolled the rotting head until she looked into its pale, dead eyes. She drew the copper knife and smiled. She didn't know if the monster at the pond could hear her, but she was confident it could see her. She waved the knife in front of the dead man's eyes.

"We are coming for you."

She stabbed down through the left eye. As the dead man's head dissolved, she stood and looked around. Seeing nothing else, she smiled at Daisy. "Shall we head back?"

Daisy nodded. "Let's go home."

FIFTEEN

The burial of Edith Harrison, the lone casualty of the attack on Tierra de Cobre, took place late the following morning. Maria and Rachel led a team of townswomen in swiftly digging the grave, rifles near to hand and one eye on the trail to the stream-fed pond. There was no undertaker to measure the body and build a coffin, so the women wrapped Edith up in blankets and lowered her into the earth.

The women and the handful of old men unaffected by the beast's call asked Elizabeth to lead a short graveside service. Edith was baptized Methodist according to Rachel, but someone needed to say some words, so Elizabeth agreed, taking the responses in the little Catholic mission to be permission to minister to the local flock until a fully ordained priest or preacher could be found. Elizabeth selected a short verse from Ecclesiastes and let the women who knew Edith best speak to the dead woman's character and memory. Words spoken, the old men took it upon themselves to finish the task and began shoveling brown earth over her body.

The rest gathered in the saloon, as it boasted a space large enough for anyone with an opinion to gather and air their thoughts. Elizabeth stood apart from the women of Tierra de Cobre. They needed to make this decision. Ophelia stood silent in another corner. Abigail took a seat at the far end of the bar. Sofia fell back on her years working in places like this and took over bartending. Kira and Daisy were nowhere to be seen. Clara, pale and drawn but unwilling to miss the opportunity to chronicle the meeting, lounged on the one divan, notebook open, pencils sharp. Elizabeth wondered how long it would be before Clara could climb the ladder to the belfry. The response to her message would not wait long.

Temperance took to the center of the room. The elderly woman's eyes swept the assembly. Her eyes lingered on Elizabeth briefly before she addressed the room. "After last night, no one would cast blame if any of you wanted to pack up and leave."

"I'm going. I'm taking my children and going," a voice called out. Elizabeth didn't know the woman's name, but the fear in her voice was easy to read.

"With the monster growing stronger, the road to Magdalena might be cut off," Maria countered.

"Folks could go north, head toward Socorro. Lots of little towns along the trail," Rachel Owens replied. "Or south, find the mail trail and follow it to safety."

"Are you leaving?" Maria asked. "You've been frank about quitting our claim and abandoning Tierra de Cobre."

"No," Rachel said. "I'm staying. I refuse to give up until the mine is cleared of the monster." She paused and looked at Elizabeth. "Unless you need to trap the demon in the mine to stop it."

"We still don't know how to destroy the beast," Elizabeth said softly.

Sofia set a bottle of whiskey on the bar, opened it, and poured the amber liquid into a glass. She tossed it back in a gulp. "We need to see the monster. See its lair, its true self."

The crowd of women became a loud, ready-to-panic mess, but before everything could fall apart, Elizabeth stood. The room went quiet. "None of you will be required to come with us. None of you are required to fight this battle. If the women of Tierra de Cobre decide to evacuate, we will do our best to guard your flight instead."

"I am staying," Maria climbed up on the bar and stared down the room. "I am staying. Rachel is staying. I know Temperance will stay." Maria glared at the other women, a challenge in her eyes. "I am sorry Edith died. I cannot promise you that we will survive, but we have so far. I say we stay and fight."

At the end of Maria's little speech, the room broke into noisy chaos, and Elizabeth was unsure how they would break. She did not know what she and her band would do if the town split and half the women decided to flee while the others stood and fought.

Daisy burst into the saloon as the angry and frightened voices reached a crescendo. "Someone's coming down the road from Magdalena. Two riders."

Quickly gathering their weapons, the women of Tierra de Cobre stepped out to greet them. Elizabeth moved to the front and stood with Maria and a few others. She noted Abigail and Ophelia had moved into position to create a crossfire.

A pair of riders on tired horses came slowly down the street. Both were women.

"Anna-Beth! Charlotte!" Maria shouted, face breaking into a smile.

The women of Tierra de Cobre surrounded their lost sisters and helped them down from their saddles. Maria hugged both women. "I thought you weren't coming back?"

Charlotte shook her head, red hair loose and spilling around her face. "We couldn't let you all face this alone. Tierra de Cobre is our home."

Anna-Beth hugged Maria. "We talked it over and realized we needed to come back. I mean, what would my husband say from beyond the grave if he knew I'd run off and left you? I'm the mayor's wife, for goodness' sake. I can't just abandon my duties."

Elizabeth should have been elated at the return and celebration of the two wayward women. Anna-Beth and Charlotte's appearance bolstered everyone's courage and strangled any more talk of fleeing. It should be a good sign.

But to her, everything felt off again.

SIXTEEN

"I'm not fond of either choice," Ophelia said. Elizabeth's reassuring smile did nothing to ease Ophelia's nagging feeling they were, as her Uncle Kennesaw used to say, trapped between the devil and the deep blue sea.

"If you want to see the beast in its lair, you must go with the scouting party," Elizabeth said. "It is a quick and simple trip to observe. We shouldn't send both people who wield magic. Sofia seems to know something about what lurks at the pond, so she and Kira give us the best chance to learn something. You are best suited to protect them while Abigail has the defenses of the town set and the townswomen confident in those defenses."

"I hate leaving you alone with everything this chaotic."

Elizabeth placed a hand on her arm. "I know. I suspect you will be in much more danger than I, at least for now. Our opponent will need to consider last night's little raid before they make another attack on the town."

"Next time, they'll come at us full force."

"Agreed. So find out how big a force we face." Elizabeth sighed. "Silence and scouting and skullduggery are your strength. Kira is adept at being invisible. And you need to keep Sofia alive so she can find the monster's weakness."

"I know. I just…" Ophelia frowned at Anna-Beth and Charlotte talking to Rachel Owens. The returned townswomen set off her inner alarms. Since they'd returned to Tierra de Cobre, they'd gone everywhere together, including, according to Maria, going to Charlotte's home each night.

"I am aware of them," Elizabeth said.

"Something is going on there."

"Yes. I feel it as well. Maria is watching them." Elizabeth's smile turned tight. "She doesn't trust their sudden change of heart to come home."

Ophelia nodded. "Okay. Just stick with Abigail if it all goes bad."

"I promise. Though I'll be joining Clara on the belfry. Hopefully, Sister Blandina will reply to my message."

"Can she help? If she decides to, I mean."

"Oh, love, the men might run Holy Mother Church, but it is the nuns who get things done."

KIRA TURNED to the women following her and waved them forward. Ophelia moved silently up and settled next to Kira. Sofia and Daisy—whom Sofia insisted they needed along—came next. Kira wished she were alone or with only Ophelia, but she wasn't consulted. It wasn't that she distrusted Sofia or Daisy, but neither of them moved as silently as her or Ophelia. Kira thought stealth was more important than either Sofia's magic or Daisy's extra rifle, even if that rifle was the Henry repeater Clara used before being wounded.

Instead, she insisted on taking the lead as they moved to the pond that the creek flowed through. Satisfied none of the other women would give away their position, Kira studied the scene below.

Several—she couldn't call them men anymore—male corpses either shambled or else stood limply in the sun. Kira counted twenty-two of them and could smell the decay from her hiding place.

Ophelia touched her on the arm and pointed. A group of a dozen men without the pallor or rot of the dead attended the woman sitting with her back to them in the pond, pouring water over her bare back and shoulders. A dark-haired woman none of them recognized moved among the living men, touching them on the face before sending them back to attend to their dark mistress. Parked nearby were a small two-wheeled hack wagon and a full-sized stagecoach. The horses that pulled either rig stood still as statues, picketed beyond the wagons.

"Is that Marshal Greeley?" Sofia asked softly, pointing at one of the men tending the beast.

"Yes," Ophelia replied. "I don't like what I'm seeing here."

"What?" Kira asked.

"One of the men tending the beast is the town marshal of Magdalena," Sofia said.

"Why on Earth would Greeley be here?" Ophelia wondered aloud.

"Maybe the marshal was escorting Aunt Anna-Beth and Mrs. Klaski." Daisy frowned. "But that would mean they've met the beast. Why didn't they say something?"

"Because they have been turned," Kira said. "They

have been made into dark daughters." She looked at Daisy. "The woman you knew as your aunt is gone."

"What do you mean, gone?" Daisy asked. "How could you possibly know?"

Kira shifted positions. "The creature cannot control women, but it can change them into one of its daughters. If Greeley was escorting your aunt and her friend back to Tierra de Cobre and they were captured, they must have been turned. Otherwise they would be dead."

"We can't know that for sure," Daisy countered.

Ophelia shifted her weight. "Still, if there's any possibility of that being true, we should head back to town. The others don't know what is walking amongst them if those women are helping that thing."

Kira frowned. She knew she should care about the women who were surely now daughters of the beast roaming the streets of Tierra de Cobre, but if the beast was now creating spawn and controlling men without killing them, it needed to be stopped immediately. Kira reached for the knife tucked away under her skirt. She could end this right now if she could reach the thing. She knew it. She only needed to slip into the camp under cover of darkness, and all this would end. Her fingers touched the copper blade.

The woman in the pond jerked as if shot. She looked over her shoulder at Kira. Kira sucked in a breath, her blood turning cold as the woman's face came into view.

Under the luxurious black hair rested a horse's long, broad skull, tapered at the end, eye sockets set back. The mouth opened, front incisors gleaming. It rose from the rock it sat upon and rose to tower over the men surrounding her.

"Oh. Oh, it *is* the Sihuanaba," Sofia whispered. "Run! Run!"

Before the women could react to Sofia's warning, the beast screamed.

The sound ripped through the countryside and washed over the women hiding in the brushes. Kira clapped her hands over her ears in a vain attempt to silence the terrible sound. Each second, the scream stretched out and drained the life from her body. A terrible darkness gripped her, and she struggled for release. She caught sight of Ophelia. The woman's eyes widened, her mouth opened, but her voice was silent, as if the terrible keening muffled all other sounds.

Kira stared back at the monster. It stood now, facing them. The possessed men began walking toward them, drawing their weapons. Kira struggled against the magic of the keening and raised her rifle, knowing she could never hope to fight off all the enemies coming toward them. Drawing extra rounds from her pouch for faster reloading, she lifted the Springfield to her shoulder and fired.

The enemy fell backward from the impact of the big round, collapsing onto its back. Kira swiftly reloaded, raised the rifle again, and fired. She missed her target, but the sharp report of the rifle broke Sofia from the spell, allowing the sorceress to act.

As Kira reloaded again, Sofia rose to her feet next to Kira, arms outstretched, a manic gleam in her eyes, facing the horse-headed beast below. In her hands, Sofia held pieces of raw copper. Kira did not understand the words she shouted, but she felt them in her stomach as they rolled over her. She swayed on her feet, dizzy.

The world went silent, so silent Kira's ears rang against the unnaturalness of it. Sofia took her eyes off the monster and frowned at the others.

"Run, you idiots!"

Kira shook her head. She would not abandon Sofia. She turned back to their foes and raised her rifle even as Ophelia grabbed the back of her blouse, yelling that they must flee. Kira fired at the monster and tried to reload.

The beast turned its full attention to Sofia, as did all the possessed men, who fired as one at her. The sorceress shuddered under the impact of multiple hits.

Daisy screamed and rapidly worked the action on her rifle, firing as fast as she could.

The monster opened its mouth again. Kira did not, could not, hear any noise. Sofia, bleeding and swaying, appeared to scream a challenge right back at the beast, her eyes wide. The lumps of copper left her hands and flashed across the distance toward the monster as Sofia Podany exploded.

The shock of the sudden demise of her friend made Kira's knees weak. She began to collapse despite Ophelia's frantic tugging. She swayed, unable to stop staring at the bloody ruins of Sofia's black dress, torn and flung into a low sagebrush. The terrible keening stopped, but the fire from the possessed minions of the Sihuanaba continued. After a moment, Kira recovered enough to allow Ophelia to drag her away from the grim scene as Daisy covered their retreat toward the dubious safety of Tierra de Cobre.

THERE IS something wrong with them, Maria thought, watching Anna-Beth and Charlotte talking to Rachel. The two women stood so close that sometimes their arms and hands touched. While Anna-Beth and Charlotte were friends, they'd never struck Maria as being so attached. *Like lovers.* Yet since their return, they had been inseparable, going as far as both women staying together at the Klaski home.

Anna-Beth never checked in with her niece, acting as if Daisy living with Kira in Anna-Beth's house was of no concern. She'd barely spoken to Daisy since her return, only when Daisy initiated the conversation. The woman appeared utterly unconcerned as a girl she'd raised since Daisy was orphaned at barely three years old, now went off scouting the lair of their deadly opponent.

Yes, something is wrong, and I will find out what it is. Maria leaned on the support post in front of the hotel. Initially, she took the return of Anna-Beth and Charlotte as a sign to stay and fight it out. Once her relief and joy at their return faded, the odd behavior of the two drew her attention. The town might be in New Mexico Territory, but white folks mostly settled Tierra de Cobre, and anyone who wasn't a member of the town's elite or one of their wives needed to be alert to the subtle signs and signals.

Once most of the men disappeared, the Mexican, Black, native, and elderly working women of Tierra de Cobre stepped up and led. Despite Anna-Beth being the mayor's wife, despite Charlotte Klaski holding a position of respect as a teacher, women like Temperance—and herself, she realized—took control, held things together in the face of death and disaster.

Speaking of signals. Maria glanced at the mission belfry. Clara and Elizabeth stood setting up Clara's machine. Clara barely made it up the ladder to the belfry, and then only because Elizabeth carried the case with Clara's portable telegraph, allowing the injured Clara to focus on the climb. As much as Clara wanted the machine kept a secret, there wasn't much you *could* keep secret in a little town. The local gossip mill was enough to make Miss Clara Dashelle's secret everyone's business. She felt confident in these women she had hired, trusted them, but kept a close watch on *them* as well.

When did you become so distrusting, Maria Garcia? She watched Clara set up the machine. The reporter turned the crank, the loud clicking sounding strange even for Tierra de Cobre. The noise caught the attention of Anna-Beth and Charlotte, who both glanced up at the belfry, startled expressions at the unfamiliar sound on their faces.

All worries at the strange reaction of the two women fled Maria's mind as a terrible scream reached the village and washed over everyone in Tierra de Cobre. Those with less steady nerves broke and ran at the sound, desperate to escape the horrible howl. They fled for cellars, closets to hide in, and beds to crawl under. A few ran away from town, past the little bits of cultivated land and towards the badlands.

Maria cringed under the weight of the sonic attack, but she held her ground, shook off the worst of the scream's effects, her sense of duty to protect Tierra de Cobre overcoming the need to flee.

She scanned the town. She couldn't see Anna-Beth, but Charlotte stood at the jail, hands on the door. Maria gasped in awe as Charlotte ripped the door off the building and cast it aside. William Clancy and Vicente Romo burst forth like wild men, William heading toward the mission. Vicente accepted a pistol from Charlotte and began trotting down the street toward the pond.

Mierda. I can't stop them both. Drawing her revolver, Maria ran down the alley to intercept Vicente.

ABIGAIL STIFFENED as the strange scream penetrated the walls and windows of the saloon. She'd been going over the best ways to protect Tierra de Cobre from the next attack with Temperance and several local women, but now her cadre of defenders began to unravel. The old man behind the bar covered his ears and dropped to his knees. Several of the townswomen did the same. Two fled outright, running for the back door of the saloon.

Exchanging a glance with Temperance, who'd picked up her shotgun from the bar, Abigail started for the door. She could hear the same screech as the other women, but it did not affect her or Temperance. *Probably because my ears ring from years of gunfire, and Temperance is old and likely hard of hearing,* she thought.

She was five paces from the door when Anna-Beth burst through it, Winchester held at her hip, eyes wide and wild, her pale face twisted in a snarl, showing teeth too pointed and too long for a human being. Abigail hesitated for a split second, long enough for Anna-Beth to fire first. Abigail groaned as the bullet smashed into her shoulder, spinning her around as the hot lead projectile passed completely through her flesh. She heard two more shots, followed by the deep roar of a shotgun and another two shots.

Determined to defend her charges, Abigail stayed on her feet, drew her .44 Russian, and wheeled to face the possessed Anna-Beth.

ELIZABETH FROWNED as the Sihuanaba's voice washed over her. The multiple layers of protective prayers and small blessed objects Elizabeth carried defended her from the mystical attack. But a quick check on Clara found she'd stopped cranking the device, eyes wide in fear.

"Keep powering the device!" Elizabeth called out. "We need that message."

"I—Elizabeth—I—" Clara took several shallow breaths but began cranking the handle again.

"The Sihuanaba's voice cannot harm you. Do not fear, Clara Dashelle." Elizabeth knew the truth: if they'd been closer to the monster, this attack could cripple or kill the unprotected. Elizabeth could only pray that Sofia protected Ophelia and the others from the brunt of the attack. *Please stay safe, beloved,* Elizabeth thought, making it a prayer. She leaned over the side of the belfry, took in the chaos erupting below her, and watched as Charlotte ripped apart the jail door with demonic strength, releasing the men inside. The younger man ran toward the mission as Maria drew her weapon and ran to intercept the older man.

Elizabeth stepped up to the hatch leading to the belfry, looking down the ladder to the church floor below, and interposed herself between Clara and the threat rushing toward them. She didn't know if he planned to attack them, but she would defend Clara the best she could.

"Vicente! Vicente Romo, stop right there!" Maria stepped in front of the possessed man, ten yards away from him, pistol held ready.

"I must join our lady," he said. Vicente glanced at the pistol in Maria's hand and frowned. He held his weapon barrel pointed at the ground. "Come with me, Maria. Come and know the love of our lady. She will gift you with powers you cannot even imagine. Join us."

"No," Maria said. His face turned dark and twisted. "Vicente, please, please don't make me kill you. Please drop the gun and come with me."

"No. I will not be caged again."

Maria stood calmly as Vicente lifted his pistol. Everything slowed around her. As the Colt in Vicente's hand rose, Maria stared down the sights of her weapon, fired once, and a red blossom of blood stained Vicente's shirt where the bullet struck. She fired again, putting a second round into his chest. Vicente's first bullet struck the ground at Maria's feet. She fired again, this time hitting him in the neck, but still he stood and fought. Her shoulder burned where a bullet grazed her. She held her ground and fired a fourth round. The bullet smashed into Vicente's face and exited out the back of his skull as the force of the blow toppled him backward.

Maria looked over the barrel of her Colt as Vicente lay motionless in the dirt. In mere seconds, she had killed a man. Killed someone she knew, someone not a walking corpse or mindless thrall. Maria dropped to her knees and began to cry at the waste of it all.

Abigail took two steps to the right, trying to reach the minimal cover of one of the big tables Anna-Beth tracked her movement and fired two quick rounds, one of which shattered the back of a wooden chair, sending splinters flying. The second struck Abigail in her left arm.

Gritting her teeth against the pain of shattered bone, Abigail returned fire, putting three rounds into Anna-Beth in a tight cluster near her heart. Anna-Beth blinked in surprise and regarded the crimson stain spreading across her white blouse.

The rifle fell from Anna-Beth's hands as she looked up at Abigail, confusion spreading across her face. "What? I don't—oh, God!" Anna-Beth's eyes rolled up, and she collapsed to the floor of the saloon.

An unearthly wailing filled the saloon. Abigail turned

to face the new danger, even as her own life slipped away from her wounds. She saw Temperance on the floor of the saloon, bleeding and crawling toward her shotgun, just before Charlotte pounced upon her, eyes wide and crazy, mouth open in something between a scream and a snarl, a large hunting knife clutched in her hand.

The blade entered Abigail's chest as Charlotte's weight and momentum bore her to the ground. The monstrous woman landed on her knees, straddling Abigail's prone body. She withdrew the knife and began stabbing Abigail in the chest with short, rapid thrusts. Blood filled Abigail's mouth as she lifted her Smith and Wesson. With unearthly strength, Charlotte grabbed her wrist, twisted and snapped it. The pistol fell out of Abigail's numb fingers.

Abigail Long could only watch helplessly as Charlotte reached down with both hands, now sporting long dark nails at the end of her fingers, and grabbed Abigail by the head. The gunfighter stared into her eyes for a moment before Charlotte twisted her neck with an ugly snap.

Abigail Long exhaled a last rattling breath as death claimed her.

Elizabeth waited for the possessed man to enter the mission and climb the ladder, unsure as to how she would stop him once he reached the top.

She glanced at Clara, who continued to crank the wireless, powering it up and preparing it to receive the hoped-for message. She heard the scrambling of feet below her and looked back down at the man, little more than a teenage boy, climbing the ladder. Elizabeth retreated a pair of steps as he scrambled over the hatch, snarling.

"Stop!" she shouted. "I command you to stop!"

He flew back as if a horse kicked him. His eyes widened as he fell backward through the hatch, crashing to the floor below. Elizabeth looked down at him. He lay staring up at Elizabeth, unblinking. She kept her eyes on him for several seconds until she decided he no longer posed a threat. A wash of grief at the senseless loss of his life, followed by a stab of guilt for being the instrument of his death, rushed through Elizabeth. She turned her attention back to Clara and her machine.

"Miss Dashelle, are we ready—"

"Behind you!" Clara screamed, pointing.

Elizabeth turned at the sound of a growl and scream. The teen boy, his head resting on his shoulder at an impossible angle, hovered in midair, obviously having leaped up from the floor below through the hatch as if death made him more powerful. He hung in the air for a split second as the mission belfry filled with light as the copper wires used to transmit and receive messages glowed brightly. His body shook in the power before it simply came apart, pieces of him falling with a wet thud on the floor below.

Backing away from the carnage, Elizabeth's mind whirled with this latest information. She knew the town now wielded a powerful weapon if they could figure out how best to use it. The retching noises behind her made Elizabeth turn. Clara leaned on the side of the belfry, vomiting over the edge of the mission. The wireless's flywheel whirled as a message printed on the thin slip of paper.

Once she composed herself, Clara translated the dots and dashes. Sister Blandina and the Sisters of Charity were already on the way to assist, along with a Jesuit Mage-Priest from Albuquerque.

They only needed to hold out for a few more days.

CHAPTER

SEVENTEEN

Maria frowned. Her shoulder still stung from the graze of the bullet even after Elizabeth tended to her wound. Now, the survivors of the last two battles gathered again.

I should have stayed closer to them. I should have done something, she thought. So much death, and for what? A part of Maria wished they'd all fled, but it was too late now. Daisy and Kira scouted the area and found the Sihuanaba's undead and possessed minions surrounding the town. The final attack was coming, and all of them sensed it. *And both our sorcerer and battle commander are dead.* With Temperance gravely wounded, the others turned to her to lead, but from where Maria stood, she would only be leading them to their deaths.

If Ophelia's report concerning the demise of Sofia Podany was true, there was little they could do to stop the Sihuanaba from destroying them all.

"We just need to hold out for a few days," Elizabeth said softly.

122

"I don't know if we can, Beth," Ophelia sat at the bar, cleaning her and Temperance's shotguns.

Maria glanced around to ensure the group of women packing raw copper into what shells they could scrounge up kept working. It wouldn't be much, but at least copper proved deadly to the possessed and could injure the Sihuanaba. Ophelia explained how when poor, doomed Sofia released the copper she held, the raw metal slammed into the Sihuanaba, knocking it flat, flame and smoke rose from the wounds the copper inflicted. Somehow, Sofia drew all the force of the monster's voice to her, allowing the others to flee, absorbing the deadly attack until her body could no longer handle the strain. Daisy corroborated Ophelia's tale in a soft, stunned whisper.

"Can we set copper wire around the town and power it with Clara's wireless?" Rachel said.

"There is not enough wire for such an endeavor," Clara said. "Could we lure them into a building we've wired?"

Ophelia frowned. "I'd be worried we wouldn't be able to lure enough of them into a building, or they'd burn it down around us."

"What we need is a cannon," Rachel said. This drew a chuckle from the other women. "We could load it with copper and just blast the damned things."

Maria smiled at Rachel. "Or a Gatling gun. Fill the air with copper bullets."

"Might as well wish for a flying pony to carry us all away from Tierra de Cobre," Ophelia chuckled.

"Now, that would just be ridiculous," Rachel said.

Maria raised an eyebrow. "You know we're being attacked by a monster able to possess men and kill with its voice?"

Rachel shrugged. "I'm just saying flying ponies are fantasy."

"I can kill the beast."

Maria turned to look at Kira. Everyone else gave the young Apache their attention. "Oh?" Maria didn't want to contradict the woman outright.

Kira drew a copper blade from the folds of her tattered skirt. "I can kill it. With this."

Elizabeth stepped up to Kira. "May I ask where you acquired such a weapon?"

"My grandmother," Kira said. "She gifted it to me before her death."

Elizabeth reached out with one hand and stopped before she touched the blade. She whispered something in Latin, and the blade glowed softly. Elizabeth stared at the knife for a few seconds, then stepped back. The glow faded.

"Well?" Maria asked.

Elizabeth smiled. "This knife is imbued with power to destroy the beast."

"I've seen it turn the living dead men to dust when Kira stabs them," Daisy said.

"Excellent," Elizabeth replied.

"But how do we protect Kira long enough so she can get close and use her knife?" Rachel shrugged.

Maria nodded. "Okay. We know they're coming. We have a few copper bullets to hand a sharpshooter, enough copper shot to load up a few shotguns, a machine to generate energy capable of destroying the possessed men, but with limited range, and Kira's magical dagger."

"We need to stop the beast from using its voice," Ophelia said.

Maria nodded. "If we can stop her from crying out, we can at least try to fight free and escape."

"We also have the mine," Elizabeth said softly. "I suspect the beast would not wish to enter, though it could send her minions in pursuit."

"Excuse me," Clara said. "I realize I'm not Abigail, but as I understand it, we need to draw the beast's forces off and neutralize her voice so Kira can attack with her magical knife, yes?"

"That's what we just said, Miss Dashelle," Ophelia agreed.

Clara nodded. "Do we know the beast's location? Is it still at the pond?

"Yes," Kira said. "When last Daisy and I scouted, the men were moving, but she remained behind."

Clara bit her bottom lip. "She won't take the field unless she must. Even though it failed in the end, Sofia's attack would make the beast more cautious. We know how to injure this Sihuanaba, and it knows we can hurt it."

Maria nodded in understanding. "We send a small team armed with copper to the pond while the rest of us keep the dead and entranced busy."

Clara nodded. "Yes. I'd suggest the pond team include Kira so she can use her knife."

"I'm worried about splitting up," Ophelia said. "Again."

"We should verify the beast still dwells at the pond," Rachel suggested.

Maria stared out the window of the saloon. They didn't know when the attack would come, but it would be soon. "Let's put the team together and let them find the Sihuanaba, whether she's at the pond or on the move."

"I should go now," Kira said. "I need to find the beast."

"We should go," Daisy said softly. The quiet teen set the Henry rifle on her shoulder. "I'm as good a shot as anyone here and better than most. I'll take some of those copper bullets if you please."

Ophelia chewed her bottom lip for a moment before passing a handful of bullets to Daisy. "You'll need to swap that Henry rifle for a Winchester."

Daisy shrugged. "I don't think that will be a problem. The general store has a couple. I'll go grab one before we head out."

"Put 'em to good use, girl," Ophelia said.

"I should go as well," Maria said. "You will need someone to protect you from any men she keeps behind."

"I'll go," Rachel replied. "The town needs you here to lead."

Maria and Rachel stared at each other for a few seconds until Maria finally nodded in agreement. "Very well. You make sure to keep them safe."

"I think three is the correct number," Elizabeth agreed. "Everyone else should stay and defend the village."

Rachel frowned. "Do you think…is there any hope for our menfolk?"

Ophelia shook her head. "Even if Sofia lived to break the hold on them, I don't think they have minds of their own anymore. The ones still alive, they looked…" Ophelia waved a hand in the air as if trying to pluck out the right word.

"They looked like puppets. Mindless puppets," Daisy said in a near whisper.

Rachel took a deep breath. "Okay. They're gone. They're gone, and we must do whatever we can to survive."

Maria nodded at the assembled women. "Yes. We fight. We fight and survive."

EIGHTEEN

Kira led her little band toward the pond, slipping past small clusters of the beast's minions. They might have been noticed, but the undead and possessed men were single-minded in their drive toward the town. It was just as well they were so focused. While Daisy moved almost as silently as Ophelia, Rachel Owens made enough noise for all three of them. If the undead did turn on them, Kira considered sending Rachel off to certain death if it would cause enough distraction for her to slip through and make her kill.

Would you be so quick to send Daisy to her death if it meant destroying the Sihuanaba? Kira took a slow breath. If she had to, she would allow every life in New Mexico Territory to be snuffed out if it saved the rest of the world. Noisy, clumsy Rachel would just be the first. *How can one woman make so much noise?*

As they drew closer to the pond, the vegetation thickened, giving them more cover. Kira guided them to a slight rise in the terrain, enough that they could look down into the pond before committing. The three women settled on their stomachs and peered at the scene below.

"There she is," Daisy whispered.

Below them, the Sihuanaba sat with her naked back to Kira and her companions. Two men tended her.

"She looks smaller," Kira whispered. "Perhaps she has been diminished."

"Is that likely?" Daisy asked.

"I saw the place she was trapped in the mine. The outline of her body was no larger than Rachel."

Daisy shrugged. "Well, if we're getting a smaller, less deadly version, I won't complain."

"Do we have a plan?" Rachel asked. "Maybe something beyond charge down the little hill shouting and shooting?"

Kira grimaced. She had not thought this far ahead, instead waiting to close on her opponent and then slip through whatever opening presented itself. Now she stood with her opponent perhaps a hundred yards away and no idea how to reach the target. Charging straight down the hill would have been an excellent plan, except the Sihuanaba would kill them all with her voice before they could cross the distance.

"What we need is a distraction," Rachel whispered.

Daisy looked over at Rachel. "Then we should supply one." Looking at Kira, Daisy smiled. "Do you think you can sneak into the camp? Or get close, and we'll do something to draw attention away?"

"Yes. That could work. Is there a way I could signal you to start your distraction?"

"I'm partial to owl hoots," Daisy said. "Okay. Here is the plan: Kira moves into a position where she can attack the monster. When she signals, Rachel and I will open fire on the two men. Lead is good enough for them, so I'll hold back my copper bullets in case we need to use them on that creature." Daisy licked her lips. "Kira, you've got to kill it before it can scream."

"I'll go for the throat."

"You've probably got one chance, so make sure you strike true." Daisy lifted her rifle and sighted down the barrel. "Off you go. Don't get killed."

Kira slipped away from her companions, heading alone into the enemy's camp. This was fine with Kira. *This,* she thought, *is how it should be.* The copper knife that was her family's legacy against the dark monster her ancestors once trapped. Kira silently prayed her ancestors would stand with her this night, prayed she had the strength to end this threat, promised *Hascin* the Creator she would trade her own life if the Creator but guided her to victory.

Kira moved into position. She would need to pass several yards of open ground and one of the men to reach her target, but it was the best place to spring her ambush. Kira looked toward where she knew Daisy and Rachel waited. Raising her cupped hands to her mouth, she called out in her best imitation of the night flyers, a single great hoot.

The results were immediate. First, the Sihuanaba turned toward the sound of Kira's voice. Kira waited for the great and terrible horse skull to come into sight. Instead, she was greeted with the face of the woman they had noticed waiting on the Sihuanaba earlier. Kira had one instant to realize they had been tricked before her companions opened fire. One of the men jerked as a bullet blasted through his shoulder.

The roar of the two rifles drew the attention of her opponents. They turned and looked up the hill. The men were drawing weapons, the woman was raising her hands, her nails growing into long talons. Kira charged across the distance, slipped past the man nearest her, screamed her challenge, and leaped the last few feet, knife in both her hands held over her head. She heard the rifles firing, but kept focused on the dark daughter.

Kira finished her leap almost in the embrace of the creature. The knife slammed into the possessed woman just under her neck and cut through flesh and bone with ease, spraying Kira in blood and bile as she finished landing on her knees. The creature howled and began to burn with a blue-green flame.

Kira rolled away from the living inferno, moved out of the pond and settled into a squat, knife low and ready to fight. She heard Daisy and Rachel rushing down the hill toward her. A rifle barked, the flash from the barrel catching her eye.

The torn, flaming creature stumbled toward Kira, reaching out with a burning hand. Kira danced out of the way as the thing collapsed to the ground, burning brightly in the night. A hot, painful sensation in her side made Kira wheel to find one of the possessed men aiming his pistol at her to fire again. Rachel leaped in front of her as the man fired again, taking the bullet meant for her. Kira readied to throw the knife as the man cocked his gun again, but neither managed to act. Stepping into the weird blue-green light of the flames, Daisy lifted her rifle and fired point-blank into the man's head. His skull exploded and his body fell, unmoving.

The fight ended as quickly as it started. The only sounds now the burning of the dark daughter and Rachel Owens' low moans. Daisy moved to Rachel, who sat up, holding her arm. Daisy worked to stem the bleeding before checking on Kira.

"Are you also hurt?" Daisy asked.

"I'm bleeding, but nothing too serious."

Rachel took a series of deep breaths. "Was that the monster?"

"No," Kira replied. She was wadding up torn bits of her skirts and holding them in place over her wound.

Daisy looked at Kira. "The real Sihuanaba must be on the move."

"Yes," Kira agreed. "I need to get back to town."

"*We* need to get back to town," Daisy said.

Rachel took another deep breath. "How bad is it?"

"Bullet went through your arm but missed the bone. I'm going to use your bullet pouch to tie this off. Kira! Where are you going?"

"The horses. We need to move quickly. The Sihuanaba is attacking the town."

Rachel looked at both women. "Go on. If you survive, come back for me. If you lose, well, I'll have to make a choice, won't I?"

Daisy fished out two copper bullets. "These should work in your Colt. Use them as you see fit."

The horses, broken from their trances, stamped and whinnied. Kira, favoring her side but determined, patted the big mare on the shoulder and looked at Daisy. "Can you ride bareback?"

"Yes. Can you rig something up to control her with?"

Kira pointed to a stack of saddles and tack behind the stagecoach, likely taken from the various bravos who had met their end at this little waterhole. "Those should do. I don't want to waste time with the saddle."

The two women slipped the bridle and bit onto the likely-looking mare. Daisy helped the wounded Kira up on the animal's back, then leaped and swung herself up behind Kira.

"Go," Daisy said, leaning against Kira and hanging on as they rode hard in the dark for Tierra de Cobre.

CHAPTER
NINETEEN

Elizabeth stood unarmed in the middle of the deserted street, presenting a tempting target for their opponents. The warm wind blew the little tendrils of hair that escaped her braids, tickling her cheeks and forehead. A small whirlwind—a dust devil—crashed into the hem of her dress and dissipated upon striking the fabric, leaving a thin coating of brown earth on her black dress. She drew her veil over her face. At her back, the little mission stood at the end of the street, door open wide.

Come and get me, she thought. *I'm just one poor, unarmed woman. Nothing to fear.*

Around her, the defenders of Tierra de Cobre waited. Some prepared to join the battle. Others stood ready to tend the wounded, reload weapons, and spring the traps poor dead Abigail Long set up. Elizabeth frowned to herself. The dead lay in the little hotel's storage room, the town too busy preparing for battle to bury their fallen. Elizabeth worried they would rise as the angry dead if left unburied too long, though the odds were they would all join them once they fell defending the town.

And who will mourn for you, Elizabeth Chapman? Who will wash and bury your body? Who will weep for your death?

Ophelia argued long and hard with Elizabeth about the folly of exposing herself where any idiot with a gun and a bit of luck might put a bullet into her, but Elizabeth needed to make her stand in this spot.

Though I shan't stay this exposed once the lead starts to fly.

In the slowly dying light, she could see the cloud of dust rising as the enemy began to move en masse. She cast a glance around the village. They were surrounded.

Well, nothing for it, Elizabeth decided, lightly touching the crucifix hanging around her neck. She prayed that Kira, Daisy, and Rachel managed to slip past the line of undead and possessed. *Let the dying begin.*

MARIA GARCIA STOOD in the gathering shadows behind the jail. She carried her husband's Colt Navy revolver in her right hand, the mail bag she had brought from Magdalena filled with small bundles of dynamite from the mine swinging from her shoulder, and a pocket full of lucifers. She watched and waited. Kira and Daisy thought the attack from this direction would be mostly the possessed men and would be the toughest battle. Around her, she heard the soft breathing of anxious women, preparing to fight, the whisper of their clothing as they shifted nervously.

I should say something encouraging, Maria thought, *but I won't lie. Not now. Not to these people.*

She could wish Abigail were still alive. She could wish Temperance did not lie dying, carried back to the little shack she called home on the edge of town, but Temperance demanded to live her final hours and minutes in the house she'd built and shared with her long-dead husband. Maria could wish for many things, all in vain. They came for her, weapons drawn and ready as they shuffled toward her and her little band of fighters. To her left, the deep roar of a shotgun broke the stillness.

Too far away to be Ophelia, Maria thought. She took a moment to mourn for Temperance, who planned to die defending her little patch with her last breath. As the attackers drew nearer, Maria raised her pistol.

"Now!" Maria cried out, and a dozen weapons roared to life, muzzle blasts lighting up the street. Maria drew her first bundle of dynamite and struck a match.

THE SHAMBLING UNDEAD, rotting and crumbling like a colony of lepers, attacked down the main street. Elizabeth suspected the Sihuanaba must be trying to induce terror more than kill or injure anyone, and she knew if another unfamiliar with metaphysical mysteries, weirdness, and monsters of the world faced this horde, the tactic would work.

It would not work against her.

As the hot evening wind rose, Elizabeth closed her eyes and whispered a prayer not found in the common canon, begging Jesus, Mary, and all the saints to defend this little town and its occupants from the undead horde bearing down upon it, praying to be the vessel of light against the darkness, though undeserving

As the first of the undead drew near, his lower jaw hanging loose, eye sockets empty, a blazing radiance erupted from out of the little mission at her back, wrapped itself around Elizabeth for a moment before tendrils of the holy light reached toward the undead horde. Where the tendrils touched, a creature would crumble, becoming dust to be blown away by the winds.

The power surged through Elizabeth. She lost all awareness of her surroundings and self, caught up in the fury of the divine energy filling her body and soul. She heard them now: the voices of all the saints and Mary, Mother of God, calling to her.

"Come home. Come home, wandering daughter."

Elizabeth wished she could, sometimes. Some days, she longed for the sanctuary and security of Holy Mother Church and missed the women of her order. But as much as she yearned for her lost life, she would never go back, would never give up Ophelia, not for all the saints and their miracles past, present, and future.

As the strain of wielding the holy light became too much for her body to bear, Elizabeth released the energies, allowing them to snap back into the mission.

"We understand, daughter," the fading voices said. "We understand and will wait for you."

As the last of the power left her, Elizabeth collapsed to her knees onto the dirt street, gasping for breath, too exhausted to flee the oncoming undead. A score or more of them lay destroyed by her hand, but still they came.

Strong hands lifted Elizabeth from the ground, half-carried, half-dragged her into the mission and settled her on the floor. She looked up. Ophelia, worry etched on her face, leaned down to kiss Elizabeth before unslinging her shotgun from her back, moving to plant herself firmly on the threshold of the mission door.

Elizabeth watched as Clara dashed across the doorway in front of Ophelia, copper wire in her hand as the dead advanced on the mission. The now familiar clicking and whirring of Clara powering up her machine and charging the wires filled Elizabeth's ears.

The power running through the copper shredded the bodies of the dead men, sending their remains into the dirt, pieces of flesh, white bones, and rotting innards littering the street.

Staggering to her feet, Elizabeth moved to join Ophelia, took two steps toward the entryway, and stopped.

Beyond the killing box of copper wires stood the beast. Over seven feet tall, it bore the shapely naked body of a woman. The head, however, was more hideous and horse-like than Ophelia described. For a long moment, Elizabeth locked eyes with the monster.

"Shit," Ophelia cried out.

A detached part of Elizabeth's brain noticed Ophelia grabbing Clara, drawing the reporter into the mission. But her eyes and primary focus stayed on the thing striding down the street toward them, watching in fascination as the abomination opened its mouth. Ophelia scrambled to shut the mission door, but Elizabeth knew the structure would not save them and would not muffle the horrible scream enough to dull the effects at close range.

Elizabeth strode past her love, mentally praying Ophelia might yet escape. She clasped her rosary, drew upon the power of her faith, and moved to meet her fate.

CHAPTER

TWENTY

Maria kept under cover as the possessed men advanced and opened fire on the defenders of Tierra de Cobre. They were not accurate, she'd discovered. Their primary tactic was to fire in unison as they advanced, focusing on one target and showering their target with lead.

Maria kept their rain of bullets focused on her, allowing the other defenders to pick off targets around the edges, whittling away at their opponent's numbers.

Scrambling from the dubious cover of an overturned wagon, Maria raced for the adobe walls of the little Catholic mission. Not so much for its excellent protection but to steer the possessed men into one of Abigail Long's traps.

The oversized mailbag of explosives flapping against her hip as she ran, Maria reached the mission. She drew her second bundle of dynamite, struck a match, lit the fuse, and threw it with all her might at the possessed men. She didn't expect the explosion to do much damage, but it would keep their attention on her and keep the horde moving in the desired direction. Maria ducked around the corner as the explosives detonated. She peered around the edge and fired twice into the mass of bodies for good measure. The possessed men turned and returned firing at her as one.

Diving back under cover, Maria glanced behind her, watching for anything creeping up on her.

A desiccated arm reached around the opposite corner of the mission. Maria flattened herself on the mission wall even as the adobe splintered and bullets whined near her. She lifted her revolver and tried to remember how many rounds were left. The Colt reloaded slowly, and she only carried a hunting knife and a .22 derringer as backup weapons. Looking over the gun barrel, Maria waited for the undead monster to appear.

The jaw hung slack, eye sockets empty except for the maggots wiggling. Tattered and filthy clothing hung from its body, showing a left hand missing, the bone of the arm showing white. Despite the terrible condition of the body, she recognized him. Before her stood the remains of her Esteban. She had accepted his fate. But now, facing this…

"*Querido Dios, no*. No. Do not force me to do this." Tears filled her eyes, and for one terrible moment, Maria wanted to quit, to let the inevitable happen and join her husband in death. The leathery tips of his fingers touched her face with the caress of the grave.

She stepped back, gasping and sobbing. No. She would not die at the hands of this rotting abomination. Maria aimed the barrel of her pistol at her dead husband's head. "I am so sorry. The Esteban I loved is gone." She squeezed the trigger.

The hammer clicked, bullets spent.

Maria lowered her pistol. For one moment, she thought surely this was a punishment from God for being unfaithful, if only in her heart. Her dead husband approached, relentless, mindless, reaching out for her. Around her, the sounds of battle broke through her thoughts. Pieces of adobe from the corner of the church broke off and struck her under a barrage of bullets.

The sudden stinging pain brought Maria back to herself. She ducked the grasping hand and moved behind him, slipping the hammer loop and drawing the revolver still in the corpse's holster. Maria stepped backward as the monster clumsily began to turn toward her. She lifted Esteban's Remington .45 and fired one round into his head. His body crumpled to the ground and withered away.

Finding cartridges still in the belt the corpse left behind, Maria reloaded both of her dead husband's guns. She pocketed a few spares and glanced at the desiccated thing that had once been Esteban. She had known he was dead. She had grieved, and though her heart hurt at what fate forced upon her, the thing responsible for Esteban's death and the death of so many others was still out there somewhere. She took a deep breath and, with a scream, ran from the cover of the mission toward the livery, firing both pistols wildly.

Now thinned by the relentless sniping from the defenders, the possessed horde turned and lurched toward her.

The first rows fell into the trench the women dug and covered with rotting wood and bits of vegetation over the last few days. A second group followed, and a third before the possessed stopped their forward momentum.

When the trap sprung, Grethe was tasked with lighting the oil and other flammables, but the German woman did not appear. Maria dug into her bag and pulled out the last bundle of dynamite. Unwilling to trust her ability to throw the bundle true and accurately, she charged forward, shooting until the hammer of the Colt Navy clicked on an empty chamber. She tossed it aside and drew the Remington, emptying it as well. The last row of possessed men standing at the lip of the pit fired directly at her. Maria stumbled as the hot lead ripped into her flesh. The second volley tore into her, and still she struggled forward, staggering.

As she stumbled to her knees a handful of feet away from the trench, she stared at the ground and waited for the third salvo from the possessed firing squad.

A pair of small, booted feet came into view. Maria looked up into the wild eyes of Charlotte Klaski.

"You should have stayed with us in Magdalena, Maria, and never returned to this doomed place." The woman smiled coldly at her. "Anna-Beth and I started back to Tierra de Cobre to help defend this town, but oh, *She* found us, gave us purpose, taught us a new way to live. You could have known Her love and power. I would have loved you and called you sister as we recreated this world in her image." Charlotte shook her head. "So much waste."

Feeling her life slipping away, Maria locked eyes with Charlotte. "Thank you," Maria gasped, blood falling from her lips, bright and pink.

Charlotte frowned and cocked her head in confusion. "For what?"

"Talking too much."

Maria pulled out the lit bundle of dynamite she'd been concealing with her wrecked body, summoned the last of her strength, and surged forward. Her shoulder took Charlotte in the stomach, both women toppling over into the pit.

The explosion and fire destroyed the last possessed men, Charlotte Klaski, and Maria Garcia.

CHAPTER

TWENTY-ONE

Ophelia's shotgun roared out in the close confines of the little mission. Clara screamed in what might have been fear or a challenge.

Elizabeth could do nothing to assist them, her every bit of focus and energy reserved for the Sihuanaba before her. Elizabeth wrapped herself in the fading holy energies sluggishly filling her body, prepared to be a light and channel unto death and to die well doing her life's work of defending the world from darkness.

Why do you strive with me, priestess of the hanged god? Join me. Join me, and we shall free my siblings, birth my children, and make this world into the paradise your young godling promised but did not create.

Elizabeth swayed as the voice filled her head. Images spooled out in her mind; images of the world turned into the Great Garden of Eden from which God cast man. She only needed to give herself over, and no more of the women of Tierra de Cobre would die needlessly. She would gather them up like lost sheep, and she their shepherd. No more would her love for Ophelia be forbidden.

141

Not because of holy vows, not because they were the same sex, not because their skin had different hues. No more tyranny at the hands of men's laws and men's interpretations of the holy word. The world reshaped in the image of this goddess before her. This goddess and her siblings awoken and reborn.

And Elizabeth would be their High Priestess, all sins and transgressions forgiven.

Yes, the voice whispered. *Come to me so I may teach you my love.*

Elizabeth took two shuffling steps, drawn to the beast's promise of power and a place in this new world. Around her, the sounds of fighting stopped.

She took another step. Another.

KIRA LEANED AS FAR over the horse's neck as possible, urging the beast to more speed. The sounds of battle reached her ears over the horse's churning hooves.

"How are we going to get past all that mess?" Daisy shouted in her ear.

"The only way in is through," Kira called back.

"That seems like a poor choice," Daisy replied.

Kira could see the monster moving toward the mission. "Are you ready with those copper bullets?"

"Reloading on the back of a moving horse isn't easy."

Kira bit her bottom lip. She had the wild thought to ride right through all the fighting, leap from the back of the horse, and plunge the knife into the beast. Which, as Daisy would no doubt say, seemed like a poor choice, the more so because Kira was wounded and struggling to control the horse. Spotting an opening in the battle, Kira turned the horse down a side street. The mare was more than happy to oblige, running in any direction not including wild gunfire or a supernatural monster.

Swinging around behind the main street, Kira waited until Daisy scrambled off the mare and let Daisy help her down. She checked her wound and decided she would hold together long enough to complete her mission.

"We'll swing around on opposite sides. I'll come up behind the monster. You need to blast it in the throat before I attack."

Daisy nodded, pushing the copper rounds into the rifle's magazine. "Wouldn't want to shoot you by accident."

"Please don't shoot me. I know what I'm asking will be difficult. I know, but you must hit her neck and stop her voice. Otherwise…"

"I know," Daisy said. "And Kira…"

"What?" Kira blinked in surprise as Daisy kissed her.

Daisy pulled back. "I'm fond of you. Don't get killed." Daisy turned on her heels and ran off before Kira could respond, vanishing around the public jacks behind the saloon.

Kira licked her lips and turned the opposite way, determined to attack the Sihuanaba from behind. She planned to slip behind the monster and cut her pale throat, hopefully after Daisy wrecked her voice.

Kira squatted down to find a spot where she only needed to dash a few yards to reach her target. She rechecked her wound. Her clothes were ruined, but they were a dead woman's clothes anyway, loaned to her by Daisy from her aunt's garments.

She studied the back of the monster, watched as the Sihuanaba squared off with Elizabeth. *What the hell is Elizabeth doing?* Kira thought. *She's just standing there swaying. No! She is walking toward the fiend.*

In the moment it took Kira to realize Elizabeth was

enthralled and imperiled, a large explosion tossed dirt and flames and the spirits only knew what else into the air. Elizabeth pulled back from the beast, alarm on her face. A rifle crack sounded. Elizabeth charged the monster.

Gathering her strength, Kira burst from her cover, dashing toward the Sihuanaba, drawing her knife as she started her leap.

THE EXPLOSION CUT through the silence and broke Elizabeth from her fascination. She clutched her crucifix and surged forward as a rifle shot filled the air. The beast twisted in pain as bright crimson blood spurted from its throat. It opened its long mouth to scream and gurgled out blood instead.

As Elizabeth closed with the beast, Kira sprang upon its shoulders from behind, wrapped an arm under the head, and pulled back. Kira stabbed with the copper knife into the Sihuanaba's exposed neck.

The monster's blood rained down onto the dirt street. Daisy, standing on Elizabeth's left with her rifle raised, fired twice. The beast toppled forward, Kira riding its back down to the bloody street. The monster gave a great shudder, throwing Kira off.

It rose to its knees before Elizabeth.

Elizabeth reached out and gently stroked the monster's bone muzzle. "This world is not for you, nor your kin." As she pressed the crucifix onto the beast's head, the monster's eyes rolled in fear. The Sihuanaba tried to cry out, but only blood passed from the mouth.

Elizabeth called holy radiance down on the thing, held firm as skin and hair, muscle and organs boiled and melted away, held firm as the beast dissolved until only an ordinary horse skull, except for the wicked incisors it bore, bleached and bare, rested under her hand. At last, the skull collapsed into the dirt, shattered. Around them, the remaining minions of the monster fell and crumbled to dust with the death of their mistress.

The survivors of the battle for Tierra de Cobre walked tentatively into the street, looking around as if they did not quite believe they had won.

Elizabeth locked eyes with Kira. "The knife would have been enough."

"I know," Kira replied.

"But I found this ending quite satisfying." She frowned at Kira. "You are injured."

"Yes," Kira agreed.

Daisy took Kira by the arm. "Let's get you inside the schoolhouse with the rest of the wounded, and maybe Miss Elizabeth here can patch you up."

Elizabeth turned to face Ophelia. "Once I'm done with the injured, I think our labors here will be complete, my love."

"Did we win?" Clara asked, emerging from the mission, derringer and knife in her hands. "Because it doesn't feel..." She waved her arm at the street, her face pale, dress covered in blood and grime.

"Like a victory?" Elizabeth finished for her. "It never does. And now, Miss Dashelle, you can report the truth. Or as much of it as anyone will hear."

TWENTY-TWO

Ophelia tightened the straps on her horse's saddle and checked the bags and packs on hers and Elizabeth's mounts. The good women of Tierra de Cobre proved true to their word. They paid in both coin and silver odds and ends. Ophelia figured they could sell the silver in the next town of any size they found themselves in. Elizabeth glided toward her, entirely too serene for someone who'd killed an old god.

"Are we ready?" Elizabeth asked.

"Yeah. You think we should head back to Magdalena and the train?"

"No. I thought we'd ride to Socorro," Elizabeth replied. "It seems a better choice."

Ophelia nodded in agreement. "I suspect Magdalena might not exactly welcome us with open arms."

"With the marshal dead, they might welcome us with a tall tree and a short rope," Elizabeth said.

The two women mounted their horses and rode toward the north. Clara stood in the street, holding up her hand to stop them. Ophelia noted the younger woman dressed like she belonged now, wearing a plain light blue blouse and heavy brown skirt—no more Philadelphia finery.

"Ladies," Clara said by way of greeting. "It has been an honor to fight by your side."

Ophelia smiled. "And with you, Miss Dashelle. And I find myself right pleased you survived to tell the tale."

Clara smiled back. "And tell it I shall."

"And are you sure this is your chosen path?" Elizabeth asked.

"Yes. I own a printing press and a share in a fine copper mine. I find myself a businesswoman. I think it will be good to remain here and help rebuild."

When everything settled, Rachel Owens, bloody but standing, took the remaining survivors in hand. With the danger passed, they chose to rebuild the town, try to sell some shares in the mine, and reopen it. Rachel and the others gifted Clara with the town newspaper and the former home of Charlotte and John Klaski.

"I feel it's time to create something of my own, and I've had quite my fill of fighting monsters," Clara finished.

"I understand," Elizabeth said. She reached out and shook Clara's hand. "Good luck to you, Clara Dashelle."

"And to you both," Clara replied, shaking hands with the two women before they parted.

Ophelia turned her horse back to the road. Around them, the survivors cleaned up their town, buried their dead, and prepared for their future. Ophelia nodded toward the mission, now under the care of a half-dozen nuns and a priest in black robes. "You sure you don't want to…"

"No," Elizabeth said firmly. "No. I've spoken with Sister Blandina, and it will be enough."

They rode past the town cemetery, past the fresh graves of the fallen. Abigail Long, Temperance Freeman, Maria

Garcia, an empty grave with a marker for Sofia Podany, and too many other women and men, earth piled high upon them.

"We won, and yet…" Ophelia shrugged.

"They won," Elizabeth said, nodding back toward Tierra de Cobre. "And we, well, we just carry on."

"Toward the next thing trying to kill us," Ophelia said. "Regrets?"

"None. Where you go, I will go, beloved."

Two riders and a mule crossed their path and trotted beside them. Kira, again wearing her battered blouse and skirt but now mounted on a handsome gelding with new tack. Daisy, dressed in men's clothing, revolver hung cross draw on her belt, sat on the mare they'd found at the pond. Ophelia thought Daisy resembled Abigail now. But she hoped the fight for Tierra de Cobre had disavowed any romantic notions of adventure Daisy might harbor from all those dime novels. That the youngster's life would be longer and less violent than that of Abigail Long.

"May we ride with you, at least for a time?" Kira asked.

"The more the merrier," Ophelia replied. "What are you two planning?"

Kira peered at the horizon and back to Daisy, who smiled back at her. "No real plan yet. Just ride for now. Sofia…" Kira paused and turned to study the graves behind them before she waved at the mule. "Sofia left a note willing her possessions to me so we might find a place to hole up for the winter and study the writings she left behind."

"There is much dangerous knowledge contained in those books and scrolls," Elizabeth pointed out.

Kira nodded solemnly. "Yes."

"Well, I think the company would be fine," Ophelia

said. "We're riding to Socorro for now. You are both most welcome to ride along."

The four women, survivors of so much horror, put Tierra de Cobre behind them. Riding beside Elizabeth, Ophelia reached out and clasped her beloved's hand.

ABOUT THE AUTHOR

Michael Merriam is a writer, performer, poet, and playwright. He is the author of the urban fantasy *Last Car to Annwn Station* and co-author, with Sherry Merriam, of *Charming Mayhem: a Six Guns and Sorcery Omnibus.* His essays have appeared in *Uncanny Magazine*, *Cast of Wonders*, and *Andromeda Spaceways Inflight Magazine.* His scripts have been produced for stage and radio, and he has appeared in the Minnesota Fringe Festival and StoryFest Minnesota. Like most artists, he has worked a variety of odd jobs over the years, including short order cook, late night radio disc jockey, international freight specialist, and manager of a puppet troupe. He lives in Minneapolis, MN with his wife and an exuberant cat and a quiet dog. Visit his website at www.michaelmerriam.com.

ABOUT QUEEN OF SWORDS PRESS

Queen of Swords is an independent small press, specializing in swashbuckling tales of derring-do, bold new adventures in time and space, mysterious stories of the occult and arcane and fantastical tales of people and lands far and near. Visit us online at www.queenofsword spress.com and sign up for our mailing list to get notified about upcoming releases and offers. Or follow us on Facebook at the Queen of Swords Press page so you don't miss any press news.

If you have a moment, the author would appreciate you taking the time to leave a review for this book at Goodreads, your blog or on the site you purchased it from.

Thank you for your assistance and your support of our authors.